The Night Is A Mouth

The Night Is A Mouth

LISA FOAD

Exile Editions

Publishers of singular
Fiction, Poetry, Drama, Nonfiction and Graphic Books
2009

Library and Archives Canada Cataloguing in Publication

Foad, Lisa, 1976-
    The night is a mouth / Lisa Foad.

ISBN 978-1-55096-114-0

    I. Title.

PS8611.O23N53 2008   C813'.6   C2008-906127-6

Design and Composition by KellEnK Styleset
Cover Art and End Paper Illustration by Sonja Ahlers
Typeset in Tribute fonts at the Moons of Jupiter Studios
Printed in Canada by Gauvin Imprimerie

The publisher would like to acknowledge the financial assistance of
the Canada Council for the Arts and the Ontario Arts Council, which is an
agency of the Government of Ontario.

Published in Canada in 2009 by Exile Editions Ltd.
144483 Southgate Road 14
General Delivery
Holstein, Ontario, N0G 2A0
info@exileeditions.com
www.ExileEditions.com

Canadian Sales Distribution:
McArthur & Company
c/o Harper Collins
1995 Markham Road
Toronto, ON M1B 5M8
toll free: 1 800 387 0117

U.S. Sales Distribution:
Independent Publishers Group
814 North Franklin Street
Chicago, IL 60610
www.ipgbook.com
toll free: 1 800 888 4741

This one's for Angie & me.

CONTENTS

Between Our Legs

On the television, colour bars are exercising. Alert. In tandem, the high-pitched attention signal, pitching. Attention.

This is a test. This is only a test.

Between our legs, we hold the difference.

How did it happen? We're not really sure. How did what happen? We're really not sure. At first we waited. And then we waved. We saw them and we stopped waiting and we started waving.

1.

We had our hair tied back. Thick shiny twists that hung like commas. Punctuation suspended – we had it tied up in our hair. Punctuation suspended – along with disbelief.

Believe me.

We had waived our ability to interrogate predictability, plausibility. Realism is for beginners. Logic is for the birds. We never did like birds. And we liked to pretend we were not beginners.

2.

Our lips were smudged in deep purple. They looked fat and swollen like hammered out thumbs. We smacked our deep purple lips in the mirror. Patted them with powder like we were patting down for guns. Copping a feel. We felt good.

We licked our lips. Our lipstick stayed on.

We fluttered our french-manicured fingers. Iridescent polish, white tips – our nails shone like opals, even glowed in the dark. All of this from a box called a kit. Do It Yourself. We did it ourselves.

Then we frenched. Our lipstick stayed on.

When we left the house, we passed the yard with the sign that says KEEP OFF. We rolled our shoulders. Our bones yawned under our skin. This is what they call a shrug. So? We kept off.

3.

We were dusted in flecks of gold glitter. The flecks fell across our collarbones, our shoulders and the blades in back. Our shoulders and our collarbones were bare because our shirts, which were dresses that were mini, were off the shoulder. Keep off. Except for the flecks of gold glitter.

The glitter came from talcum powder. The talc, called Gold Dust – what else? – came from a box that came from Glo's mom. Inside the box were ends, archiving the thing that had ended: a can opener; two crumpled silk dress shirts; a sliver of spicy soap-on-a-rope; a hammer. And, of course: seven thin gold bracelets; a near-full bottle of Giorgio; Gold Dust; notes and cards that swore, *Sorry*, and, *I'm so sorry*, and, *I love you*.

There was no underwear in the box. Sisco didn't wear underwear.

The day Glo's mom threw him out was the day she found him in the bathroom, Glo pressed between his shiny black-slacked legs and the wall. From the doorway, she'd spat, "Goddammit, Sisco. Goddamn you," her blue feather earrings fluttering softly as she shook her head slowly from side to side.

He reached for her, clucking his tongue and the word "baby," but her hands found him first. "Get. Out." KEEP OFF. And she slammed the bathroom door, locking him out and her and Glo in with the purple and gold magnolias that papered the walls.

"Shit." She reached for Glo's earlobe, gave it a halfhearted tug. Sat herself down on the lip of the bathtub, knees knocking at the toilet. And then, feathers trembling, she bedded her head in her palms and she cried.

When Glo saw the box of leftovers that her mom left curbside the next day, she grabbed the Gold Dust and made a run for it.

4.

The breeze swirled its way round our bare legs, up through our minidresses and around our necks. Our teeth chattered. Our nipples poked through the thin cotton. We wrapped our arms around the cages of our ribs and cupped our breasts with our hands. We were cold.

5.

We were waiting and then we were waving.

But before we were waving, when we were still waiting, we'd tried to look nonchalant, without purpose. We smoked cigarettes because we had some. We put our hands on our hips. We said, "fuck," a lot. We tried to look bored. Bored silly. We tried to look like we belonged on the block. Like without us, the block was just a block. Just bricks. Just sticks. Just bricks and sticks and stones.

But our ears were burning. Something fierce. And in our heads, it was raining. Cats and dogs. So we did what we could to manage. We covered our ears. We shook our heads. We shrugged. We tried not to want the things we wanted: to look nice; for someone to look at us nicely; for someone to worry because they cared; to not care either way. No way.

We were holding it, this longing, between our legs so no one would see. Yet, someone saw. Two someones saw. The ones for whom we were waiting, the ones to whom we waved saw. We'd seen them lots before. But it was only last week that they looked back.

INTERRUPTION: MILES & WINSTON

We saw. They were waiting right where we'd told them to wait – on the corner with the all-night convenience store. Shifting their weight from foot to foot. We saw them see us. We saw them wave. We saw their cold parts and their warm parts. We saw where our hands belonged. We saw that it wouldn't be long.

Their faces crinkled up when they laughed. We felt our faces crinkle up whenever theirs did. They laughed at everything. We laughed at everything. So that on the walk back to Winston's house, we were four sets of spreading smiles, balled-up cheeks, squinting eyes.

Their dresses hugged at their hips, pulled across their chests, tugged low off their shoulders, and you could almost see. But we didn't want them to see. So we kept it between our legs. For later.

We liked the way their bodies sloped and curved. It made us want to risk things – concern, comfort, the security and safety of borders. It made us want to enlist in a cause greater than ourselves.

See, their stomachs scooped inwards like they'd been hollowed out. It was like they were barely there. Like something was missing: drive or care. Like they'd give up easily. On their studies. Their plants. Their parents. Like they'd been given up on before.

We didn't give up.

6.

We liked the way they looked at us. Liked also, the way they said our names. *Sophie. Glo.* Their voices were weighted with things like matter. We felt ourselves materialize in the thinness of the air.

And we fell. Over swirling blue drinks in highball glasses. They caught us. They caught us by the necks. At first it felt so good we didn't feel a thing.

Suspended.

We had our hands tied like bows. Behind our backs, we did not fight back. There was nothing to fight.

Believe me. There was nothing to fight.

Interruption: Miles & Winston

I think they were smiling the whole time. But we couldn't really see their faces. I guess we didn't really care. I didn't much like the one's face. It was angular, her jawline extreme. Sophie though, I very much liked her face. But once I'd seen it, it was with me and it stayed. I didn't have much use for looking again.

I guess we caught them by surprise. I guess they didn't see it coming. I guess their expectations might have resided elsewhere. Like when you take a sip from a glass and expect Coke but it's iced tea or some other mix up. You flinch, you make a face, you think about spitting it out. But then you realize. Now you know. So you just let go. They really let us go.

They were smiling the whole time. We could tell because their lips were stained deep purple. I guess it could've been blood.

Like I said, they really let go. They really let us go.

7.

We were in the room with all the ugly pastel paintings. The paintings were of flowers rendered in angular brushstrokes. Flowers that also come in plastic, those fake flowers that people put in big black vases in their front halls because they feel that the feeling given off is one of slickness.

The rug was worn bare like it was barely there. We were barely there.

The walls were papered in a rosebud print. From where we were, the rosebuds looked like tiny little eyes. Millions of them. We felt them in all sorts of places.

No, we didn't feel anything at all. No, we felt like nothing.

Across the dark that was the room, our frenched nails glowed at each other. Buoys. Beacons. Searchlights. Stars.

Interruption: Miles & Winston

We had them by the hips. We had them by the hair. We had them by the wrists. They didn't say a word. They didn't have to. They dug into us, fingernails searching. Their searching said, *Find me*. We found them. Hands behind their backs, they didn't fight back.

Dead Air

Our tied-up, bowed-up hair is knotting. Our necks, shoulders and the blades in back, too. Our stomachs are clenched. Our fists, too, so that our nails, balled up in our palms, are feeling for lifelines. Trails. Traces.

In the space between the space that's this room, we are hanging. Suspended. Behind our backs, our hands KEEP OFF. There is Gold Dust everywhere.

In our heads, there's a pushing and a pulling. We think we should just stop thinking. We think if we just stop thinking, everything will be fine. Suspension of punctuation, disbelief.

For fuck's sake. It's nothing.

This is just a blanket. It's crumpled like eggshells. This is just a floor. Banging into my head. It's thinking, *Stop thinking*. It's thinking, *Let go. If you just let go, you'll get it.*

In our heads, there's nothing but static. There's nothing but snow. Poor resolution. Colour bleeding. Colour bars.

This is a test.

This is a test of the Emergency Broadcast System.

This is only a test.

We had waited before we waved. But after this, we won't wait. We won't wave. We won't say a word. We'll roll over. We'll tug the skirt ends of our dresses that are mini, down. We'll tug the shirt ends of our dresses that are mini, up. And we'll stand. We'll suck in our stomachs. We'll bare our eyes like teeth. And we will look straight ahead.

We will see without seeing. We will be seen without seeing that we've been seen. No, we won't see back. No, no one will see.

And we'll walk out the door, into the night. Down five blocks, six, the most direct route home. Keeping off grass, out of streetlights. We will not break our stride, a sweat. We'll wonder what to say. Nothing. And once we get to the street that's just past that street, we'll make a left. Slip the key in the lock and twist. Turn on the television.

What happened?

Nothing.

INTERRUPTION: MILES & WINSTON

We did it twice. One. Two. There was so much to do. I guess we fought a bit, Sophie and I, Winston and Glo. Over geography, topography. Development and yield. Limits, perimeters, margins. For things like jurisdiction and management. But we did it twice, so it's pretty obvious.

BARS & TONE

After, we didn't say anything. We got up, surprised ourselves.

But look at us. With our sucked in stomachs and our unseeing eyes, our knotted-up hair and our purpled lips. Our self-sufficient gait, our conviction. And leftover, still some Gold Dust. I guess that we're tough.

We're not really saying much. We've not got much to say. Did you do it? Yep. Did you do it? Yep. We did it. Who cares? Did it hurt? We won't say. We won't even ask. What's on your face? It looks like blood. Who cares? Let's talk of other things. Let's not talk at all.

We did it. It's ours. No one can take that away. This way, we are on our way.

After all, it's easy to fall. The difference between the things you want and the things you don't want is slight. You can have anything you want. You just have to believe that what's happening is what you want. You just have to believe that what you want is what's happening. Or else entire landscapes lift at their edges.

They didn't do a thing. We did it all ourselves. And we held it, this thing that's a brick that was once just a block, us waiting, between our legs so no one would see. No, no one did see.

Lost Dogs

Take me with you. I didn't say it. The television did. Just before we fell asleep.

You always have the TV on. You like the way its murmurs feel. Low hums that hug. Churn the air. Mark it with matter. Make it matter. There are words everywhere. They swirl and stick. Between your fingers, the clamp of your jaw, you feel letters like *i* and *d* slither and squish. Scream. You say sometimes it makes you dizzy. Sometimes it makes me dizzy.

When we wake, it's to the sound of breaking news, children gone missing.

From the knot that's our legs and arms, you disentangle. Rub at the sleep in your eyes. Prop yourself up on an elbow. Yawn.

Behind you, Mindy Lynn is missing. Seventeen hours. Last seen leaving school (gold-starred spelling test, Velcro sneakers that light up, bouncing red bursts). A blue Ford Taurus. Or was it a Toyota Corolla? It might have been a wagon. Witness this: Amber Alert. Medicine Hat, Alberta, with its cliffs and coulees.

Eleven is an average age.

Strewn beneath us, the deck of cards. In particular, we've been sleeping on the suit of spades.

You stretch out one leg taut, then the other. An inadvertent scissor kick.

On the television, a fifth grade Picture Day photo. Ringlets and red bows. Eyes, typically blue. Flush-cheeked, beaming. *Cheese.*

You fix two mossy green eyes upon me. Kohl-smoked. Real shiners.

Parents are pleading (a loose french braid, a purple hoodie, sequined blue jeans). *I can hardly breathe. I can hardly see.*

And you tell me that you are a missing child.

I find the seven of spades, use it as a visor.

Your hair is a waist-length swarm of long-legged spiders. Your t-shirt is thin and your throat is a runway.

I laugh.

You laugh.

I laugh again.

You arch your feet. "Well." Point your toes. "I was a missing child." Smile.

"What were you missing?"

You shoot me a wry look. Collect the strewn deck. Palm out for the seven of spades.

I surrender.

You shuffle slowly. Suggest, business.

I follow suit. "You're not missing anymore?"

You abandon the deck. Sit up and tail your hair to the side, drag your fingers through the knots. Say, "I'm 26. I pay my rent. I have a Visa. A Bay card. I frequent bars and movie theatres, sign up for special deals. I exist above board. I'm evident. Evidence, in fact. When you're that visible, you can't still be missing, can you? At any rate, I still feel missing. And I've tried to recover. The things I missed out on, the things I miss. It's just not the same."

You were in search of your mother.

"Isn't everyone?"

"No."

Your mother left you. She left you at the grocery store, in aisle seven, canned fruit to your left, marmalades and jams and jellies to your right.

When you were discovered some time later, you were pale and fantastically silent, a cliff. Green eyes slush grey, cheeks icy. You clutched the handlebar of the shopping cart, two tiny pink knots. Your heels, wrapped in purple velveteen booties, knocked rhythmically at the cart's steel spine. Your lips trussed, a crimson bow. Inside the cart were Ritz crackers, two tins of tuna, diapers, Cream of Wheat. She never bought Cream of Wheat. You let out your first wail only after the woman with the red florets of hair, blue checkered vest, pin that promised, firmly, in ticker tape, MANAGER, pushed you past the instant potatoes, the soups that *eat like a meal*, to the Courtesy Desk.

You tell me this in a voice that churns. Your mouth's a tilt drum mixer. Slabs of sentence, sentencing. It's a matter of fact.

The day she left you, your mother wore the smart burgundy heels with the skinny spines, sharp toes. Matching leather purse, slender shoulder strap. The burgundy blouse with the classic high neck (wrap tie, collar knot), glossy buttons. Tight designer jeans, creative back pocket stitch. Her hair fanned her face in soft, dusty waves.

"You remember all this?"

"It was in the police report."

Your father found you on the news. You were a purple velveteen ward of the Crown. In fluorescent-lit rooms with ecru-coloured walls, you'd been passed around. Fed strawberry puree. Offered apple juice, a sippy cup. At six o'clock, you were held tightly in the arms of a stranger. While you knocked your booties and gnawed on your fist, a man with a microphone pointed and *tsk*ed, pointed and *tsk*ed. The camera panned, zoomed. You buried your head in yellow silk, choked on the woody bouquet of Halston, and threw up a little. The camera tilted, zoomed. Caught the white-pink pulp as it dribbled down your chin, mashed against yellow silk, a wet scar.

The next day, the newspaper headlines boasted, MISSING CHILD, FOUND.

"So you weren't missing. You were left. Missing by default, maybe. More like misplaced."

"No." You flex your palms. Rattle your wrist, let your watch slip back into place. "I'm not done."

Your father picked you up immediately. Predictably, he couldn't even look at you. He began watching the news obsessively. Weather, especially. One night, he smashed the TV and never replaced it.

Before long, a busty woman named Marilyn with mudslide eyes was sitting at the kitchen table. Cloudy liquid wrestling with lemon slices, clunking cubes of ice. Skinny pastel cigarettes, lush strands of smoke streaming and pluming. Mounted under the corner cabinet, the mini black-and-white television (*Like sands through the hourglass... so are the Days of Our Lives*). *Non-negotiable*, she'd insisted. From the bedroom, soft murmurs. Low hums that hug, they fit together like spoons. He'd acquiesced.

She'd mix you fake drinks – oranges, reds, finger-swirl – and talk about art. Rubens, Kahlo, *The Garden of Earthly Delights*. One day, just drunk enough, she told you that your mother was either dead or in a big city with tall buildings and insufficient park space. Maybe somewhere on a television. She slid a shoebox across the table. Inside were old snapshots (honeymooning in Niagara, Happy Birthday from a mix), news clippings (bold headlines, MOTHER ABANDONS, and such), a wedding band, an engagement ring (pear-shaped solitaire, *vena amoris*). A letter. From a television station. Noting, *We were very impressed with your reel.* The location of the audition – weekend weathergirl – was blacked out. She left two days later. Whispered in your ear, on her way, *Today, the sun will suffocate beneath cloudy drifts, barely evade the drench, glassy shards of riling rain. Beam, some time later. I love you.*

"You remember this? That wasn't in the police report."

You left shortly thereafter. Eleven, average. Thumbed your way to a motel called MOTEL with a restaurant called RESTAURANT, a low-slung, brown-bricked, highway-side affair, fluorescents sizzling. You stood in the parking lot for a minute, mesmerized by the paved arteries, the barrelling headlights. Felt you'd fallen off the edge of something. You groped wildly, arms flailing. And fell. A man caught you. He was smoking a Dunhill. He told you his name was Dad and that your real name was Darling.

He took you to his room and fixed you a whisky and Coke. Threw on a motel porno. Smoked a cigarette. Took a swig of Jack. Said, *You're a real knockout*. And asked you to sit on his lap. He felt your nipples through your shirt and asked to see them. With his hands on your hips, he jiggled you about. He felt hard and it felt good. He asked if you'd ever seen a penis and you said, *Yes, the neighbour's*. He took out his penis and began to stroke it. Asked you to give it a whirl. When you touched it, you felt fiery and strong.

You repeated everything he asked. *Dad, can I go out? Dad, can I have some money? Dad, when a boy wants head, should I give it to him? Dad, what's head?* You knew he wasn't really your father. Because your real father didn't feel this good.

He let you suck on his penis and taught you how to take it all the way down your throat. He spread your legs and, with his penis in his hand, helped you find your clit. When he finally got his cock in you, it burned so bad and you felt so good. You fell asleep in a heap. Woke once with him inside you. Woke later and went for his penis. Sucked it every chance he'd let you. Later, much later, he began to cry. You asked for a dollar for the pop machine in the hall. Bought a Pepsi. Felt your thighs twitch. And never went back.

It was in the parking lot that you met Doe.

You heard her before you saw her. Laughing. It sounded like a song you'd heard somewhere before. It made your stomach hurt. You reeled. You reached. You found her. Standing in front of the restaurant, smoking a cigarette with one of the waitresses. She was the blonde in the tight stonewashed jeans, red scoop neck t-shirt, a can of Tab and a pack of Players in hand. You tucked yourself in behind the jutting front wheel of a big rig and tried to remember the words.

Hers found you first. *Shit!* Eyes wide, sparkling green shadow. *Shit.* She picked at her cola-spattered t-shirt, dabbed at the droplets that glistened from the fleshy curves of her cleavage. She began to laugh. *You scared the shit out of me.* Her gold hoop earrings grazed her shoulders. *Excuse me, darling.* She nodded at the driver's door, turquoise rabbit's foot dangling from her key ring. *I've got to get going.*

You stuck out your thumb.

She studied you for a minute, and asked what kind of trouble you were in.

You told her you weren't in any, but that your mother might be. That she'd left you with your father who was not one. That you needed to get to a big city with insufficient park space, that you needed to find and be found.

She considered the pale yellow bruises that blotted your wrists, the whisky blear in your eyes. She said, *Hop in.* Bundled you in blue flannel and asked if you were hungry.

You were already asleep.

You rode with Doe for days. You rode with Doe for weeks. Derby City, Bull City, Motor City, The Swamp. Cigar City, Cow Town, The

Nickel. You'd never have guessed there was so much to see. For a time, you forgot that you were looking for your mother. Doe fed you fruit pie and cherry soda at every stop. She let you use the CB and blast the air horn. She told you that *hammer down* meant go faster and that *clean shot* meant no cops. Sky everywhere, you'd never felt such boundlessness.

One day, over blueberry pie at a greying rest stop, you told Doe about the man in the motel. She got so angry that you started to cry. You wondered what you'd done wrong. She squeezed into your booth seat and held you so tightly you thought you might die. It felt almost as good as the motel bed. You would have been happy to die.

She said, *We've got to go to the cops.*

You bristled. You panicked. You said, *Please, Doe.* You said, *I'm sorry, Doe.* You gripped her arms and begged. *Clean shot. Clean shot.*

She said, *You're not in trouble, darling.* She brushed your bangs out of your eyes. She nuzzled your ear. She kissed your forehead.

You never saw Doe again.

While she was in the bathroom, you bolted out the door. Mudstone sky. You never looked back.

You thumbed your way through miles and miles. This car. That car. The men who picked you up gave you hits off their joints, sips of their king cans. *Do you like ZZ Top?* they'd ask. And turn up the volume. Push your head down between their legs. *How about Zeppelin?* they'd ask. And pull over. And pull you on top of them. *Oh, that's so good,* they'd say. And thrust faster and faster, harder and harder, while your tits bobbed at their hungry mouths.

When you finally saw the skyscrapers, your eyes lit up. He leaned past you, popped open the passenger side door. Put twenty bucks in your hand and told you to take care. Sped off, just as you were swinging the door shut.

You blinked. Disoriented.

The city was dark and ridden with reeds. Cobwebs stretched from spire to spire. Gun shots. Car alarms. Burglar alarms. The hookers yelled at you to get off their fucking corner. You got off the corner. Cars careening, you nearly got hit. Billboards. Flashing neon lights. People throwing bricks and the bones they'd broken through shop windows. There was shattered glass everywhere. Music pulsing. Women screaming. *Rape. Fire.* Then not screaming at all. The sidewalk spit up on your shoes. Teenage boys with black eyes and knife-scarred jaws leaned into you, said, *Hydro. Crystal. Ice.* Men grabbed at your ass, tugged at your tits and your hair, tried to shove you down alleys. Lead pipes. People bleeding. Begging. Shivering. A car slowed down. *Get the fuck in.*

You flattened yourself against the crumbling bricks of a building, covered your ears. And began to cry.

Someone snatched you.

You opened your eyes. The brightness burned, blinded you briefly. You blinked. She had thick chin-length curls, hot pink lips. And her nametag said Bev. She pulled you. Down the length of the diner with its black and white checked floor, its red vinyl counter stools. Past the men licking gravy off their fingers, shovelling forkfuls of lemon meringue pie into their mouths. And pushed hard at the door to the Ladies'.

Your t-shirt was stained. Your eyes were bloodshot. You stank of Budweiser. And your hair was tangled, sticky with come. She said, *I've been where you've been.* And amid the fizzle of the fluorescents and the ceaseless flush of a weepy toilet, she gently leaned you over the sink. She washed your face. She rinsed your hair. She ran hand lotion through its wet tips. She gave you leggings and a leotard, an off-the-shoulder sweatshirt. She said, *I'm sorry. It's all I've got.*

When you came out of the bathroom, Bev sat you down in a shiny red booth and gave you a plate of fries. You told her your name was Darling and that you were looking for your mother. You pulled out the tattered picture you'd been carrying and slid it across the table. *Have you seen this woman? Maybe on a television? Forecasting the weather?* She hadn't. But the diner had a satellite dish. Bev gave you the remote control and let you look for your mother for days.

You channel-surfed. You canvassed the customers. You played checkers with the waitresses – Annie and Della and Guinevere. You played cards with the cook, Vance. You modeled the sparkly boa Bev gave you. You ate peach pie and key lime pie, cherry pie. You got comfortable.

One day, the cops came looking. You spied them just as you were coming out of the restroom. Stroking their nightsticks. You dropped to your knees and hid behind the cigarette machine. Watched Bev hesitate, bite her lip. And point. To the booth in which you'd been sitting, the television you'd been watching.

You slipped quietly out the back door. And ran. Past the broken glass of bus shelters, the wild spurt of unruly fire hydrants, the televisions and toasters that had been hurled off balconies, the faded posters looking for lost dogs. You ran through alleys and backyards and junkyards, up and down skinny side streets, past thin houses with bed sheets for curtains, yellowed yards, spindly trees trimmed with toilet paper and underwear, faded holiday decorations. You ran until you couldn't run anymore and curbside, you doubled over, heaving.

Dizzy, you crawled through the grass towards chimes that tinkled. Marigolds stirred. You closed your eyes. You rang the bell.

She had long honey-coloured hair and the softest voice you'd ever heard. Tears welled in your eyes. She bent. The thick gold cross that hung from her neck stung your breast. She reached. You vaulted yourself into her arms and she carried you inside, her hands stroking your hair.

Inside, everything was plush. And gold. The couch. The drapes. The flocked wallpaper. The air smelled like lemons. And everywhere you turned, tiny crystal animals – swans and seahorses, tigers and unicorns – twinkled. She said, *In the paradise, you will have one of each for your very own.* You didn't know what she meant.

You crawled up through the soft spot between her thighs. She held you. You cried and cried. She rubbed your earlobes and told you that it was okay. She braided your hair and told you that it was okay.

She said that her name was Gail and that she loved you.

She kept you. You wanted to be kept.

She poured you a glass of flat ginger ale. She ladled you a bowl of chicken soup. It made you feel like you had the flu. You snuggled into her arms. And told her you were looking for your mother. You pulled out the photograph. She said, *Let me put this somewhere safe.* She gave you a book of bible stories. Closed the gold drapes. And said, *Don't answer the door for anyone.*

You didn't.

One day, you got a horrible cramping.

Gail stuck her fingers deep inside of you and pulled out a baby. The baby was you. The baby was yours.

"So you're missing a child?"

"The cycle is like any other," you declare. "Vicious."

There was blood everywhere. She gave the baby to you to hold. You didn't know how to love. You passed out.

When you woke, you were lying on the bathroom floor. Naked. Sunlight streamed through the skylight. You squinted. And saw Gail, her bare body pale and doughy. Cross gleaming. She bent over you, hoisted your limp body to hers. And plunged you both into the icy waters of the yellow bathtub. You screamed. She said, *I'm sorry*. And, palm to sternum, she pushed you underwater. You flailed and railed against her, came up gasping and crying. She slapped you hard. Your head spun. She said, *I'm so sorry*. And held you down until there was no more fight left in you. Lifted free of the water, your lips were blue. Your head lolled. In the distance, you heard her voice, soft and pale. She said, *I'm sorry. I'm so sorry. It had to be done*. You passed out.

When you woke, your tits were swollen, leaking milk. And your whole body ached. In your abdomen, a horrible cramping. The ballerina that sat atop the toilet tank stared. Arms reaching. Her gold tulle skirt concealed the extra roll of toilet paper.

Gail eyed your weeping breasts. She said, *Don't worry. They'll dry out in no time.*

The baby was gone.

Gail told you that it would be best if you didn't leave the house. That strangers would climb inside of you and lay eggs. That the eggs would hatch snakes, and that the snakes would writhe. And eat you from the inside out.

You were terrified.

Days passed. Weeks passed.

You grew restless and bored. There was no television. There was nothing in her cupboards and drawers but unsharpened pencils and rosary beads. There was nothing to read but your book of bible stories. You couldn't find yourself anywhere but right where you were standing.

One day, you asked Gail for the picture of your mother. She said, *I'm your mother now.*

Days passed. Weeks passed.

You thought about your father. You wondered if your mother missed being a mother.

Mostly, you missed Dad. You missed being Darling.

You began to stick things inside yourself. The thick handles of knives and hairbrushes and serving spoons. Mop handles and shampoo bottles. Eggplants. You reached for whatever you could fit. And with your hands at your clit, you came and came and came.

One day, Gail, home from work early, found you fucking yourself with jars from the spice rack. She tore the bottle of paprika from your pussy and threw it across the kitchen floor. She ripped the cross from her neck. And rammed it up inside of you, smacked you so hard across the face that you came. Enraged, she hit you harder. You passed out.

When you woke, you were in the basement. Gail was crying. Chanting. *Ab omni hoste visibili et invisibili et ubíque in hoc sáeculo liberetur. From every enemy both visible and invisible and everywhere in this lifetime be freed.* One hand on a bible, the other worrying her rosary beads. Your eyes burned and your skin crawled. Her voice got louder. *Ut quóties triúmphum divínae humnilitátis, quae supérbiam nostri hostis dejecit. How often the divine humility has triumphed casting out the pride of our enemy.* You began to gag. You gave up. You gave in. She said, *Good girl.*

She bound your breasts. She cut off your hair. She stuffed stale wafers into your mouth. She said, *I'm so sorry. It had to be done.* And then she locked the door.

Days passed. Weeks passed.

Every morning after Gail left for work, you tried the door. Defeated, you hauled yourself down the stairs, back into the blackness of the basement. One night, however, after she brought you your dinner, Gail forgot to turn the key. In the morning, the knob gave to your twist. You tiptoed through the house. In the bathroom, you looked in the mirror. You had no idea who was staring back at you. You pushed hard at the front door. Sky everywhere, your knees buckled. You remembered that you'd felt this feeling of boundlessness before.

You stole a pack of Dunhills. And walked for blocks and blocks.

Somehow, you wound up in front of the diner. Vance gave you a hug and told you that Bev was long gone. Something inside of you sank. He slid you a piece of pie and asked if you wanted a job. He said you could live at the diner. Your nametag said *Darling*. One day, Vance pulled you aside and said, *There's a way for you to make more money*. You already knew how to make more money. You did it on your breaks out back with the customers. Vance called you a slut. Hauled off and hit you. He said, *Some girls are just made for this*. And hit you again. He said that he deserved a cut. And left you bleeding on the floor.

You picked yourself up and you ran.

You slept on street corners and in bank machine vestibules. And with men who had daughters, men who had wives, men who had money. You slept with women who reminded you of your mother. You slept with women who reminded you of yourself. You spent holidays at the discount cinema watching second-run movies.

You phoned your father once. You could feel him groping for hope and his glasses. You didn't say a word. You held your breath and listened. Marilyn had left him. You could feel it. The empty space in which he was sitting was so loud. He said, *Diana? Is that you?* You were looking for her, too. You had nearly forgotten her name. You hung up. Hammered the receiver against the payphone. And turned on your heel.

You walked right into Bev. She had a black eye and was digging through a dumpster. She didn't recognize you. You were sure she was Bev. You couldn't be sure. You gave her a smoke and lit one for yourself.

You aged. One year. Two years. Three.

This is how you learned to love: *It will be over soon.* This is how you learned to love: under assumed names in small rooms with bad lighting; on street corners and in alleyways, on cat-pissed couches and in bathroom stalls; the word *sorry* in your ear, over and over, *It's over.* With a wooden spoon up your pussy, slick fingers that smelled like roses. Weather poetry. A hand around your neck, sticks in your ass. This is how you learned love.

You have never found your mother. Your father found you once.

You were working at a bar called BAR. It was small and dark and it smelled like sorrow. The tap beer was warm and pale. The hard liquors were fluorescent, blue and green. All along the walls, wildlife heads, mounted: moose and bison, elk and grizzly, bobcats and cougars. Your customers were named Clyde and Moe and Cheetah. You flashed your tits often and they tipped real well. Sometimes, you'd grind hard against the bar stool till you came. You didn't ever worry about the men getting out of line. A trio of yellow-eyed wolf dogs roamed the bar, guarded things.

One day, a man wearing a ragged overcoat came in. You knew he was your father. You could see it in his grey-green eyes, the dark circles that rimmed his sockets. You could see it in the wrinkles that creased his forehead, in the downturn curl of his lips, the way he took his glasses on and off.

You poured him a pint. You slid him a shot.

He said, *I used to love a lot of things. And I used to understand. But I've lost a lot of things. And nothing looks the same. I used to have a daughter. I used to have a wife. Now, I don't recognize myself. And I'm sorry for everything.* He swirled the beer in his glass, his eyes shiny and wet. He said, *I dream of paradise often, but when I wake, I can never remember what it looks like.*

Everything inside of you came crashing down.

At the end of the night, you locked him in and you fucked him hard up against the bar. The glasses rattled. The liquor bottles smashed. The wolf dogs howled. And in his ear, you came hard again and again and again. *Darling.* You knew he would come back, the next night and the night after that. You never went back. It satisfied you greatly to know that he would spend the rest of his life looking.

"Then what?"

"Then nothing."

You stopped looking for your mother. And you stopped looking for yourself. There was nothing to find. Things get boarded up and go black. There's nothing but weeds.

You look to me, your eyes narrowed, wet. And you reach.

This is called home. Love fuck. You say, "If I don't know any better, I can't do any better." I dry your eyes. I begin to cry. We are wet and dry. We fuck through it. You say that you want to protect me, me to protect you. From wind and yourself.

Blue-white, the television glows. Low hums that hug. *Take me with you.* We do it again.

Here There Be Monsters

The package is unmarked, an amnesiac. Bandaged in stiff brown paper wrap. It sits handsomely, smack dab, on the giant mahogany dining table. Lending purpose.

"I bet it's a stopwatch," says Jed. He claps twice for emphasis.

"Nonsense!" Mother drags a limp-wrist through the air, concludes the flight palm-up: a blasé *hello,* a lazy *don't shoot.* "It's the size of a tumour."

"But I've always wanted one." Jed claps twice more, *encore!*

Mother shrieks, "Satan!" and souses Jed with the last of her Manhattan.

"My eyes!" he screams.

"My thighs," Jet murmurs. And through the thick black bangs that blunt her eyes, she watches the cherry make a run for it; a lewd dash down Jed's thigh, a sticky red skid mark, post-maidenhead.

The cherry rolls to a rest. *Whew.* And, *That's it?*

Jet disappears. Under the table, all fours, she stalks the cherry. Courts it briefly, socks it in her mouth. *Yeah, that's it.* Surfaces.

From the china cabinet, father's collection, tiny heads floating in formaldehyde, looks on disapprovingly.

"You know how I feel about clocks and watches and ticks and tocks, keeping time, and time in general," Mother chops. "As long as you're under this roof, you're more likely to get a tumour. Now get me another drink."

"I bet it's a pair of roller skates," says Jet. "I prayed for some last night."

Mother rolls her eyeballs, harrumphs. "Suck-up." With great pizzazz, a legion of headless horsemen galloping up her throat, she summons some phlegm and spits the gob, reddish-gold, at Jet's feet.

"Hurrah!" exclaims Jed. "It's positively stunning! Sun on the cusp of setting!"

"Jed, you've always been my favourite." Mother twines the wands that are her fingers through his thick black hair, until the beast that's an anniversary diamond gets caught: trap jaw, spike teeth. Mother tugs. No give. Annoyed, Mother yanks with all her might.

Jed screams bloody murder.

"Give an inch, they take a mile!" she plows, and adjusts the french cuffs of her blouse, her attitude towards xenotransplantation.

Jed begins to sob.

Father's collection is unmoved.

"There, there," she pats his cheek, a tangled lock of hair dangling from her anniversary diamond. "For God's sake, you're seventeen years old!"

"Dear God," Jet entreats. "Please forgive Mother for taking your name in vain."

Mother quarries through her rocks glass, pelts an ice cube in Jet's direction.

But Mother has terrible aim.

Jed whiplashes, takes it in the eye, begins to cry.

Father's collection stifles a giggle.

Mother sighs. "It was an accident. Throw it at your sister." And, stroking the pilfered lock of hair, she surveys her young with meaningful ejaculation: *Sweet Jesus.*

"I can see your lips moving," Jet declares. Lips, indeed. Mother's lipstick stains the outskirts of her mouth like some sort of menstrual accident.

Mother is bored to death. *Where's the beef?* She cuts her kin a real blackout of a stare and staunchly drags a first-class red spike fingernail across each wrist.

"Mother, if you really want to kill us, you have to slit vertically."

Mother's not fazed. "Jet, you need a haircut. You look like your father."

Father smiles. "I need a haircut, too." He gnaws heartily at a mouthful of uncooked rigatoni. Father's a ghost.

"Maybe it's a bomb," says Jet, and adds an extra *t* to the spelling of her name.

"Nonsense! Who would send us a bomb?" Father bellows. He's hard to understand. Post-mortem, he can't project like he used to.

"You've no idea the enemies I've made." Mother narrows one eye and hatches a sinister set of fish lips.

The hideousness is bewitching. Mother looks at her best in this room with its black velvet flocked wall covering, heraldic lions, forepaws raised, claws bared.

Mother makes that face, the one that suggests she is calculating. "Twelve."

Mother can't count. But she's a formidable guesser. "I guess no one's home." *Bingo, Mother!* "I guess I'll have seconds." *Bingo, Mother!* "I guess I'll retire now." *Bingo, Mother!*

A small voice interrupts. "It's fir me! It's fir me! It's my birfday!"

Heads swivel, father's collection included. Settle on the dog, Henrietta. *Blink. Blink.* Can't be! She hasn't said a word in two years. But Jesus, she's a knockout!

Mother feels a tug at her ankles and violently high-heels it –"Damn rats!" – across the room.

The crash is a real sweetheart, replete with the shatter of glass, the scurry of small rodents.

From the corner shadows, Jimmy emerges, forehead bleeding. "My birfday! My birfday!" He shakes off bits of glass, squeals gleefully at the multifarious refractions of light.

For a second, everyone has a good laugh.

"Oh, Jimmy, it's just you!"

"You gave us quite a start!"

"Feel that! Heart's still racing!"

"You scared the living daylights out of me!" Jazz hands. Father impales himself with a fire poker. "Scared stiff!"

Chuckles abound. Father's a real wisecracker. Even his collection is in stitches.

Jimmy dodders over to the table. Bloody. Luminous. Breathtaking.

Father's collection begins to weep.

Mother's jealous. "Take off that damned lederhosen. You've been wearing it for days!"

Jimmy giggles. Keyed up. Hands wagging. Head bobbing. He points at the package. "It's fir me! It's my birfday!"

Mother's cock-jawed with incredulity. "What do you know? You're only seven, plus you're half dead. It's like you're not even here!"

She looks to Father for support, but he's digging through what's left of the pasta. "Aha!" He holds up a perfect rigatoni noodle, models it before the light. And, with vainglorious flourish, pops it into his mouth. Crunches.

Mother clears her throat.

Father gets it together. Twists his moustache tails. Nods agreeably. And supplements, "Jimmy is half dead."

Jimmy has a tumour.

"But it's my birfday," Jimmy wails.

"Aren't you a sob story!" salts Mother.

Father's collection concurs.

Henrietta, too. She turns up her duchess of a nose, shakes her blonde Afghan mane, and sighs. *Typical.*

Meanwhile, little mister misery's a real mess, fisting tears out of his eyes while mucus bucks its way up his throat. *Cough. Cough.*

"But it is his birthday." Father removes his silk top hat, roots around, scares up a pack of gentlemen's club matches. "Here you go, Timmy. Happy birthday."

Jimmy beams. *Heaven is a place on earth.* And scuttles back to his corner.

The chandelier shudders.

Jed follows suit. And adds an *i* to the spelling of his name.

"Copycat," Jett thwacks.

"Copycat," twins Jedi.

Jett pulls her chair closer and leans in. The two mash lips, french kiss.

Mother clucks. "Not at the table!"

Jett sticks out her tongue.

Mother follows suit.

Jett flips Mother the bird.

Mother follows suit.

Jett mounts Jedi and moans.

Mother rolls her eyeballs. "You win."

Jedi feels up Jett's fantastic bosom. One perfect breast falls out.

Father's collection swoons. *Jackpot!*

The chandelier whispers, *Here there be monsters*. A crystal teardrop plummets, lands atop the package.

And the room's swathed in the brightest of orange light.

"Jimmy's caught fire!" Jett points, giddy with delight. "Oh, the gaiety! How carefree!"

Jedi claps. Mines for Jett's other perfect breast, *gold!* Goggles briefly. Thanks god for this glorious set of knockers. And feasts.

Father cheers.

His collection follows suit.

"Drop and roll!" goads Mother. "Drop and roll!"

The flaming ball continues to stumble, inebriated circles.

Mother shakes her head, thoroughly unimpressed.

The velvet lions claw furiously at the walls. And the chandelier begins to hail, a paradise of crystal teardrops.

"Damn it!" Mother marches over and shoves the blaze to the floor, rolls it about with her gold spike heel. Turns her head back to the brood at the dining table, palms cradling disbelief; the ebony switch dangles gorgeously. "For crying out loud! Do I have to do everything?" And winks at Father.

Father follows suit.

Jedi pees his pants.

Father follows suit.

Jimmy's lights go out. *Finally.*

"Now look at you." Mother can't believe her eyes. "You're filthy. And you stink. Go take a bath." She rolls him, toe-heel, swiftly away, *head start*. Returns to the dining table and thrones herself. Pauses. Nosing the air. "Now what's that? Urine?"

Father's collection gags.

Henrietta follows suit.

"Jedi and Father peed their pants," spills Jett.

"Again?" Mother's fed up, categorically cloyed. "Good for nothing, the lot of you."

Jett sniffs her armpits and says, "I smell." Laces up a pair of so-called roller skates, and pushes off. Knockers knocking.

"You're all going to hell," swears Mother. She pauses, wishing for a bon-bon. "Mark my words."

From his urine-sopped pants pocket, Jedi extracts a so-called stop-watch. Winds up.

Mother sweeps the table, arrests a fistful of crystal teardrops, and discharges. "Satan!"

Father, munching another noodle, offers Mother a thumbs-up.

This time, *curses!* Jedi takes it like a man.

Jett bestills her beating heart. But knockers are knocking.

Mother gives up. *Who gives a hoot?* And reaches for the package. Stiff brown paper wrap, *handsome devil!* "Oh," she purrs. "I almost don't want to know."

Father's collection braces itself.

It's good to know what's behind you.

Expulsion, For Emetophobia,

1.

You ask me what aftermath feels like. Swallow.

Your t-shirt swears *Mepps #1 Lure*.

Bait and tackle. I believe you.

2.

Once, I wondered about malevolent angels. We discussed their capriciousness, cut-eye. Insistent visits. The walls were sweating. You felt brave and stole a painting for me. Folk art. No one, not even the bartender, wondered what had been there before.

On our way home, you decided to go for it, so I went first. Opened wide. You rammed your index finger down my throat and toyed with my uvula, a bold acknowledgment. Until I gagged and you wilted, withdrew.

"Okay, okay, okay." You inhaled deeply. "I think I have to go first." Knelt. Eyes squeezed shut, breathing barely.

I cupped your neck. Tulips bloomed along the tracks of your throat.

As far as you're concerned, nausea is a sigh, a screech, a really good fuck. Ubiquitous.

You never can tell.

3.

Your sister's art show, eight years ago.

"No, wait. That's a lie. Two years ago, I choked on a fry at Burger King. And a little bit came up."

Spit. *No.* Swallow.

Stacked monitors. Looping signal.

People mulling. Mining for artistic intent.

Your sister wore green fishnet stockings, classy black pumps, an engagement ring made of Scotch tape. Ignored your father's inappropriate jokes, sticky laughter, moist eyes.

You drank too much wine and threw up uncontrollably in a poorly lit stairwell. On your hands and knees, lurching through inclement contractions. Your eyes crossed, as stars. You nearly recognized yourself. You nearly looked away.

Your father boarded the Greyhound, finally.

You held on. Fingers splayed.

4.

On the subway, you stare hard at small women wearing pink kitten heels, thin white belts. T-shirts that say *UNO*.

Each time someone coughs, you don't. Swallow.

We move down a few seats. And a few more. Get off the fucking train.

You never can tell.

On my way home, I cut through the car wash like I always do. Wonder if I'll get raped like I always do. Wonder. Like I always wonder.

You never can tell.

5.

I send you pictures, Samsung to Nokia. Small violent squares, reds and yellows. Still swirling. This city is a landmine.

Every abject effusion is an aesthetic triumph. Infatuating. Compelling both your gag reflex and emphatic self-discipline. Too much is enough.

The best shot, collective favourite. With its rage of pinks and heat. Across the street from Coffee Time, well into the all-night gallery walk.

What is it with art shows?

I got so close I nearly mistook it for my own expulsion. These anatomies of preservation: *L.F. was here*, and *I miss you*. Apocryphal. The pathology is mine.

Hearts are small gatherings, displacements that ripple and swell, plunge and scour.

6.

We're starving. Smear butter on late-night bagels. Lazy fingers. Greasy eyes.

I write you a poem:
Foul vile love.
Our discontent.
Wicked.

Chewing, words. Chapped lips. Swallow.

7.

On the telephone, you make noises that approximate heaving. Letters churning, words storming, tidal surge. In place of displacement, however: disavowals. Cresting, madly. You say, "It's the curry. And, Yesterday, Virginia threw up in the bathroom."

8.

In the swallow of dark, we are sightless visionaries. Shedding faculties. False attribution. Categorical mistakes. Choking on armpits and excess. Huffing words like *fuck* and *oh, god*. We ripple and swell. Spit. *No.* Swallow. *No.* Plunge and scour. Hold on.

Peripherals dizzied. *Are we there yet?* According to the semicircular canals of our inner ears, we're still moving. See, anastomosis belies endpoints.

Recognizance is disorienting: *motion sick.*

You pull hard, eyelids over eyeballs. Run for the door. And trip every time, sneaker toe caught on a door lip.

Later, you call me to say, "There is water everywhere."

I believe you.

Violent Collections, Anxious Supplements

VIOLENT COLLECTIONS

On my way into work, the black-lettered byline touts, RED HOT EROTIC NUDE LIVE! UNCENSORED VIP COUCH DANCING. WELCOME MOLSON INDY FANS. Gold-plated brick exterior, a pocketful of cascading neon stars, and a girl – she lights up one leg at a time.

"Working hard to keep you hard," says the DJ.

ABSOLUTELY NO TOUCHING. $10,000 FINE, says the sign at the back of the bar. It's nestled between a plastic potted plant and a cylindrical aquarium bearing floating faux fish.

En route to the change room, the baby blue hallway walls are littered with sloppily stencilled metallic stars. Gold and silver. Chipped tips. And housed within the belly of each star, a name. *Misty. Sapphire. Jasmyn. Jewel. Justice. Nikki.* Bubble letters, *i*'s dotted with hearts.

And we are a sky and the sky is the limit.

My back is always straight. My lips are always dewy. And my nipples are always hard. I always lean in. My back arches perfectly. I bend over with aplomb. The winged blades of my shoulders ache from feelings like flying. My spine is a beacon. Each vertebra whispers and clicks open, clicks shut, like thirty-three doors or memories or ongoing moments.

I'm a topographical wonder. Intonation. Incantation. Intoxication.

And a customer says, "You have found yourself a fan."

I keep their business cards. Vice President of Sales. CEO. Model & Talent Scout. I slip them into my purse along with palmfuls of $20s. I tell myself that one day I'll make art out of these slim slips of cardstock. An intricate mosaic, alternately glossy and matte, minimal and garish, proffering mythological certainties – perimeters, locular inhabitability, the simplicity of a clean break. There are, however, no such separations. Only pools of space.

The graffiti on the brick wall outside my bedroom window says, BOYBANDS SUCK. GIRLS SUCK BETTER. TITS RULE.

The sign outside of the church I pass on my way to the subway station says, IN THE DARK? FOLLOW THE SON.

A sandwich board on the sidewalk en route to the thrift store promises AID TO WOMEN. My friend Lil tells me it's an abortion clinic, kept quiet to avoid protests. When I ask how she's sure, she pauses and says, "The protestors."

There is some debate, however. Rumour has it that the abortion clinic is a few doors down, that in fact the AID TO WOMEN is a Christian offering for ladies who don't know any better. And Maggie's, support for sex workers, is located on the same small stretch of real estate. Here on this corner, the options for women in need are endless. And I wonder, if I stand on this corner long enough, will I get confused? And suddenly every step is suspect and every suspect is a door.

When I was six, my aunt took me downtown. I waited outside while she went into a store. When she came out, she scolded me. "Hasn't your mother taught you anything? Don't stand still. You'll look like a hooker." She taught me how to pace sidewalks with certainty, to always look like I had somewhere to go, even if it was just in circles.

Hesitation has gotten me nowhere. And I can only think in bullets, a string of directives:
Eat, or you'll faint.
Hail the first cab you see.
Don't talk to strangers.
Invisible deodorant does not glow in black light.

And these are the spaces that make framing and composition possible. This is the sky, and the sky is the limit. And I love the way my hair falls across my eyes the most.

Anxious Supplements

At home, I twist the locks, secure the windows, draw the curtains, turn out the lights and sit quietly. I wonder, can anyone hear me? I numb my lips and tongue with Listerine. Rub my shoulder where the bone sticks out. And check for a dial tone, a pulse. Call someone. I'll call anyone.

And at work, a customer says, "Come back to Chicago with me. I'll take care of everything."

And I keep everything. Save everything.

Old cassette tapes, airplane vomit bags, keys that no longer open anything, love letters. A handheld alarm and a giant safety pin with which to alternately deafen and prick potential attackers, both city-specific gifts from my grandmother.

Sometimes I tuck my hair behind my ears, furrow my brow, and attempt to dispose of the notion that objects house sentiment. These nostalgic returns yield nothing, not a thing.

The heart-shaped crystal bowl from my sister is not my sister.

It's not even an adequate representation of her – she despises decorative ornamentation and avoids glassware. She fears spontaneous cracks, wayward shards and puncture wounds. That something tragic will happen to someone she loves. Plastic cups and avoiding streets that start with the letters *J* and *S* are preventative measures.

Today on the phone, she tells me that I am irrational, that I can't keep saving things.

I take out the trash. Return the empties. Chain-smoke. Pen my name in blue ink, house it in the belly of a star. Read my horoscope. It says, *Watch for clues*.

And later, in the midst of throwing out the heart-shaped crystal bowl that is not my sister, I stumble, fall, and accidentally slit my wrist on a shard of glass. I bandage the wound with toilet paper and Scotch tape, but it bleeds profusely through the tissue. I cry for help. Try to be a good friend. And wonder things like, in which room do I look best?

At work, everyone looks good, even the floating fake fish. We are black-lit heartbeats.

And a customer says, "You don't belong here. You've got class. I could take you anywhere."

Desire is a multi-pronged instrument of restless promise. Promising alleviation. And I am, bruised from the pole, shimmering with sweat, a vision of potential, capability, culpability. This is the story and it goes on and on.

And a customer says, "I bet you're always horny. You come and come, don't you?"

Though bound by the inevitability of its failure, desire is caught within the arrogant mythology of its capacity for success. And it does not tire.

And, *Hi. Hi. Hi.* I'm a double, *baby.* A triple, *baby.* I am the supplement, supplanting. I am the insurance, ensuring. That the ontological joke is no joke.

I write notations on their business cards, tiny reminders dated in blue ink. This one wanted to fly me to Philly for the weekend. This one gave me stockings. This one thinks my name is Starr. This one tried to stick his finger up my ass. This one spent $800. This one bought us champagne. This one brought his wife.

All of them say I am different. All of them think they are different. I told them so, and so it was. I tell them so, and so it is. This is the art of collaboration.

From my purse, I retrieve a breath mint. Lips and tongue numb.

Apotheosis

I lick my lips. I look away. I don't look away. Bound and out of bounds. I am a field of flowers. Azaleas. Lilies. Chrysanthemums. Violets. *Pick me. Pick me.*

And a customer says, "I know what you want. I can see it in your eyes."

Sweetheart. I am leaning on the hood. Digging through the trunk. This is love. This is not love.

And a customer says, "I'm just across the street, the executive suite."

Baby. I am leaning on his shoulder. Digging through his pockets. This is love. This is not love.

We close our eyes and pretend that these economies of desire have no tangible currency. Co-conspirators. Together, we shape the real thing.

And a customer says, "I want to see you come."

And in the privacy of the darkened VIP lounge, with him sunk low on the leatherette loveseat, I promise and deny, promise and deny – *jouissance!* For here, something is always missing. The mark. The matter. The money shot. The evidence of affirmation. Within this endless postponement, the necessity of faith is tabled.

IN THE DARK? FOLLOW THE SON.

Later, at home, my roommate and I are interrupted by a faint whining or humming.

"What's that noise?" I ask.

She adjusts her baseball cap. Says, "What noise?"

"Don't you hear that?"

We perch quietly in the kitchen, waiting for clues.

"I think it's a car alarm," I say. Dig an apple out of the fruit bowl. And discover the handheld alarm from my grandmother, whining and humming.

Grey

There are Dos and there are Don'ts.

Do get more boxes than you think you'll need. Do use effective supporting details. Don't use toilets as trashcans. Do know the exact time. Don't try to push dislocated bones back into place. Do impress the judges. Don't call So-and-So. Don't move. *I do*. Don't. Don't. Don't say another word.

Cherry doesn't.

It's the alarm that does the talking. *Fire.*

Startled, Cherry makes a run for it. But panic draws circles. And the boxes stub and snag and stab, the wherewithal still packed. Probably in one of the twelve marked Miscellaneous.

Cherry stutters and spins out. She squints, the search for self-evidence, something with which to direct herself. But here in the heart, there is no substance. There are only suggestions: Knickknacks, Dishware, Bathroom, Fragile.

Heart racing, Cherry pauses.

There is square footage. There are walls. There are windows. There are doors.

Architecture is indisputable.

Cherry races herself to the door. Cops a feel. Hot? Cold? Who can tell? She palms the knob and pauses. Giddy shivers. She pinches her cheeks. Tousles her hair. Cinches her belt. Tongues for tooth fuzz. Licks her lips and smiles. *This is it.*

All her life, Cherry's waited for something terrible to happen.

She turns the knob.

The hallway is empty, tight-lipped, save for the bawl of the bell.

Cherry wonders if she's dead or dreaming.

Despite the lack of smoke, of flames, she narrows her eyes, plumps her rack, and does her best to romance danger while she throws open the emergency exit.

The back lot's nonchalant. It gives Cherry the once-over and yawns.

Smokestacks. Stadium lights. Slim-limbed wind turbines. Graffiti. Railroad tracks. Rainwater pooled in the yard's gaping cavities. A wolf dog bent on wresting a sheet of plywood from the shallows.

The look of emergency is often inconspicuous.

Cherry, lone beacon, sits her ass down on the fire escape. Its rusted iron slats yield suggestively.

Sunlight shimmies, bejewels the building's backside. The windows glint and swagger. They stink of arrogance and aftershave.

Cherry blushes.

The windows stiffen. Stroke their jaws, the swell in their jeans. Wink.

The knot at Cherry's knees loosens.

That's right, nod the windows. Teeth grit, hands full.

Cherry moistens.

All fired up, they model commotion. *That's right*. It's sweaty and its sound is a slur that stinks of chlorine and Trans Ams and god. *Oh, god*.

The trucks arrive in minutes. Hot red whales, wailing their way down the block.

Cherry clasps her crotch. Closes her eyes. And feels furious urgency bloom in her mouth. *I am an evacuee.*

All her life, Cherry's waited to be saved.

She cups a keen ear, anxious for the feel of heavy boot steps, hoses.

But the fire bell's exigent bleat falls silent.

Cherry gulps as matter plummets. Her lips lose their pink. Her feathered fly-backs falter.

The windows cold-shoulder.

The wolf dog wins.

The quiet swallows the quiet.

The hot spell between Cherry's thighs cools.

The sky reddens then purples, a plum.

Cherry nurses her stubs and snags and stabs. Inside her head, someone is screaming. She looks away.

There is promise. There is the end of the affair. And there is the ubiquitous grey. There is nothing like the grey.

Cherry hauls her ass inside.

Dullsville. She can't be bothered with the lights or the spooks.

Past the boxes, the bluff of substance, the belief in something special, is the remainder, which is more of the same. It bears the asymmetry of lack and its heart doesn't beat so much as it gropes.

Cherry heads for the south window. Heart groping. And drags a dispirited finger through the muck that mires the glass she has yet to clean. PLEH.

Outside, Cherry is the girl with the body. "Hell, yeah!" yell men with moustaches.

"Does this work for you?" Cherry inquires. And gives them the finger. But inside Cherry, the scraps stir and, buzzing with anticipation, leapfrog their way up her throat screaming, *I do! I do! I do!* Cherry swallows them back. Hard.

The night is white. A storm of sparks that burst and blind, spill stars, trail tails. Fucking firecrackers.

Cherry mashes her lips against the view from the south window and swaps spit with the snug feeling of hermetic sanctuary.

She knows that if she were to step outside, she'd probably get murdered.

It's a good thing she's hidden the front door. Boxes marked Bedroom and Spices and Art and Audio/Visual occlude entrances, exits, and odds.

Nonetheless, Cherry can't stop chewing her fingertips. Something is about to happen, she's sure of it. The trouble is, she can't distinguish between culpability and credit.

The fire bell suspects, and decides to settle things.

Cherry stiffens. Digs her nails into her kneecaps, fidgets with her fifty-fifty: *Am I clairvoyant or criminal? Sorry? Or spotless?*

The sofa snorts, sniggers.

Cherry shrinks. Stomach sinking.

There are eleven hot seats in this apartment. The sofa, the wing chair, the toilet, the rocker, this spot, that spot, and so on. The sofa is the worst.

Because there are the rights, and there are the wrongs.

Cherry's always wrong. And Cherry's always sorry.

Mostly, Cherry stands. But the hot seats are dogged. They can sniff out the wrongs a mile away.

Cherry balls herself up underneath the east window and waits for the whales. *This is it.*

The sofa and the fire bell squeal. Cahoots.

It wasn't me. I was at the racetrack. I was at the salon. I was at the ballet.

The sofa and the bell jeer. Exchange vows.

It was an accident. It wasn't my idea. I had to do it. They had a gun and the gun was loaded. I was not in my right mind.

The whales whine. Close in.

Cherry claps a hand across her mouth and, breath suspended, counts to three. Sufficiently shut up, she covers her ears. Buries her head in a labyrinth of limbs. And stashes herself in the shelter of elsewhere.

The sofa and the bell get hot and hump. Roll over, exhausted.

In their wake, sticky excess and bathos.

And silence.

And in behind the silence, is the squall of fireworks.

And in behind the rapid stutters, the cracks and whistles, the rash of light, is Cherry.

There is the feeling of suspension.

The grey swallows the grey.

There is the feeling of not feeling.

And there is a knock at the door.

Cherry terrors. Twists and tangles. "There's no one home!" And hands-and-knees it to the sofa for cover, comfort, a candy or two.

Once, Cherry lived with Mum. Every evening at 5 o'clock, Mum would slop supper onto chipped china and tell Cherry to move it.

Cherry was not allowed to sit across from the buffet, because the buffet was mirrored and because Cherry had a staring problem.

In the ornate wall mirror she has yet to hang, Cherry stares at her problem.

Bug eyes. Lungs clogged with the creeps. Humdrum. Foul-mouthed. *Sorry. My mistake.* Swollen glands. Boxes. Boxes. Boxes. *This sucks. That sucks.* Thumbs for fingers. Wishy-washy. Scribbles.

Small tits. So-and-So. No guts, no nothing. Moody. *Mine.* No idea. *I can't.* Bad manners. *But.* Bad luck. *But.* The only. Without tact or talent. Disqualified. This arm. That arm. Debris.

Mum says, "Rococo!"

No matter. The beauty of the single rolling tear is absolute. Cherry eats her heart out.

Mum says, "Gag me with a spoon!"

No matter. Cherry's thoroughly enamoured. There is this teardrop. There is that teardrop. The soft, deliberate blinks that yield just one stray at a time. There is the biting of the lower lip. The blur. The bloodshot. There is the glassy wet. The salt. Those cheekbones. The waste. Its weight. *This is it.*

The fire bell, kindred spirit, concurs.

Cherry falls to the floor, wills it to give.

The ceiling is a bully. The pipes, the joists, knock Cherry about. Threaten to concuss. Force her to crouch and crawl. Cramp. Lay low.

Up here, atop the loft, there are four feet of clearance at best.

Cherry shovels off her jeans and pulls up her sports socks good and tight. Sleep, and the ceiling, circle. With thumbs and forefingers that double as tacks, Cherry pins back her eyelids. Beholds the bully.

Dust clusters spider its pipes. Rusted hooks protrude from its joists.

Cherry's heart hangs itself.

Emergency. The fire bell declares it such and so it is.

Cherry dials So-and-So. "I miss you. I don't. I like you. I don't."

The fire bell corroborates.

"This bed feels like it's mine. I don't want to touch anything but me."

The fire bell substantiates.

Cherry chucks the phone. It lands somewhere in a pile of something.

So-and-So is out with someone else.

Cherry imagines stabbing someone else. And So-and-So. And so on. *Fuck. You. Fuck. You. Fuck. You.* She blows her bangs out of her eyes, grinds hard against her hands. *I'm on fire. I'm on fucking fire.*

In boxes marked Odds & Ends, Oddities, Accessories, All Sorts, Random, and Last Minute, Cherry's been up to her eyeballs.

No nothing.

She'd know it if she saw it. It would tie up her tongue and make her insides quiver. Thwart her ability to eat. Compel her to apply lip-gloss. Call her things like *Sweetheart* and *Doll* and *Angel Tits*. Give her reason. The fever. Finish her sentences. Make her feel pornographic. Perfect.

Cherry hurls a tin of tuna at the fire alarm. "You're it!"

The quiet is the sound of the flap of a thousand tiny wings.

Cherry picks a fight with the piece-of-shit stove that the last tenant left behind. And a box marked Fragile. And another box marked Fragile. The television. The radiator. The sofa. *Hell, yeah.*

The remains sparkle then stop. Dullsville.

The grey always wins. Pleased, it pats itself on the back. And says, "You're still it."

Cherry scowls and looks away.

The grey says, "Don't be such a sore loser." It gives Cherry rabbit ears and guffaws.

Cherry whacks, a ruthless elbow.

"Ouch!" The grey gives its shoulder an exaggerated rub. And leans in with a piece of advice. "Don't confuse desperation with desire."

Cherry slumps, defeated. And finds a fishhook on the floor. It's hitched to a stretch of fishing line that's spooled snugly around her ring finger.

The fire bell begins to throb, paroxysms.

The grey looks Cherry in the eye. "Do know your escape route."

Cherry nods. Takes a deep breath. And baits the hook with promise. *I do.* She cracks open her jaw. And casts.

The scraps bite immediately. And promptly engage Cherry in a violent tug of war.

"It's a live one!" the grey hollers.

Cherry jerks the line and yanks. The scraps hit the floor with a thud. Kicking. Screaming. Her insides gape. Relieved of weight. Cherry assembles the scraps into neat little rows and leans forward, gives a listen.

This one wants cupcakes! That one wants a taco! This one wants a mum that's not Mum! That one wants a blowjob! This one wants to win a contest! That one wants So-and-So! This one wants to believe! That one wants to be believed! Be good! Belong!

Don't. Don't. Don't say another word.

The phone rings.

"Hello?"

"Is it safe to come up?"

"No."

"Well, shouldn't you come down?"

"No." Cherry hangs up.

Newsprint. Cherry rubs the wrinkles out of inky sheets that once girdled glassware. And carefully swaddles the scraps.

A box. Cherry dumps the last of its leftovers. And gently stuffs the squealing bundle inside.

The phone rings again.

Cherry flips shut the flaps and, with packing tape, muzzles the box. One pass. Two.

Into the answering machine, Julia heaves her headache. "For fuck's sake, Cherry. I just talked to you. Answer. The fucking. Phone."

With a marker, Cherry crosses out the word Fragile.

June

June. June. June. He calls for June. He calls everyone June. *June.*

She gives him the finger and slams her bedroom door.

June.

She picks up the ringing telephone. "Hello?"

Her voice drops. Breathy. She threads the telephone cord through her fingers, twines it around her wrist. She saunters, a voluptuous aimlessness. Lolls against the pantry, long legs idling. She leans in to the receiver. She laughs. It's throaty, coarse with crushed rocks. It skins knees.

Lazy steps. Long vowels. She uncoils the cord. Suitable slack. She fingers the latch. And pushes out into the sun-soaked yard with its blushing lilies.

The screen door slams behind her.

June.

She says, "Edie, pass me the peas."

I pass June the peas.

His fork is poised, a stringy sliver of beef dangling from its tines. His pale lips parted. Fish eyes, bulging. He searches June.

Vivian says, "Edie, stop staring."

I stop staring.

He says, "June, would you pass me the salt?"

June doesn't.

I pass him the salt.

He pushes the fork to his lips. Chews slowly.

June lifts a hand to the side of her face, screens out his groping. "Would you stop fucking staring at me?"

Vivian says, "June! Jesus." And titters nervously.

"Jesus is right." He smiles, amused. "June, I'd wash your mouth out but I don't know where it's been."

June takes a sip of her diet cola. And tells him to go fuck himself.

"For God's sake, June!" Vivian shrieks. "Not tonight!" Her awkward fists, stray thumbs looking for a ride, hammer the table. The dishes stutter. "Can't we just have a nice goddamned dinner?" She rubs her temples. She says, "Edie, stop playing with your food."

I eat a pea.

"I'm just wondering," he says, voice plodding, eyes fixed, "if June's ever been french kissed. Have you ever been french kissed, June?"

She throws down her fork, slams her chair into the table, storms out of the room.

"June!" Vivian calls, kneading her napkin. "Don't you want any dessert?" Her eyes glitter wetly. "It's just so fucking hot in here." She lights a cigarette.

June.

"I'm not June," I say. "I'm Edie." And hand his plate to Vivian.

She plunges it into the sink full of sudsy water along with the rest of the dishes. Scrubs. Muttering, *goddamn* this and *goddamn* that. Hasty passes through the hot water rinse. The dishes clatter as they hit the rack.

He says, "I'd like a slice of pie."

"And you." She abandons the hissing rush of the tap, the tufting steam, and snaps her head round. "Always trying to get a goddamned rise out of her." Her voice is a shrill tumble. "Leave her alone."

"A rise," he laughs. "A rise."

She stares at him. Turns back to the sink. Mashes the palm of her hand against her mouth, chafes. Lets the words fall silently into the dishwater. Twists the taps, exchanges hot for cold, fills a glass. Sloshes it before him along with his pill.

And cuts him a piece of pie.

June.

In her bedroom is the difference between here and not here.

Vivian knocks. "Honey." Tentative. "Would you turn it down, please?"

June doesn't.

Vivian gives up. The kettle's whistling. She fixes herself an Earl Grey, adds a shot of whisky. And sits her ass down at the kitchen table. The blue light of the television floods through the cutout that looks onto the living room and dances erratically about her shoulders. "Jesus." Hands cupping her steaming mug. She says, "Vegas or bust."

I nod.

June.

She changes the channel. She changes the channel. She changes the channel.

Vivian sighs. "Answer Garret when he's talking to you. And get your feet off the table." She returns her attention to the purse through which she's been digging. "Edie," she holds out a crumpled bill. "Run and get me a pack of smokes, will you?"

June.

"She's gone out," I say. "It's Edie."

Seated in the gold armchair in the corner. He leans into its soft shoulder, turns his head towards the window. Fingers the sheers.

I try to be more like June.

I pull the shoelaces out of my canvas sneakers. I cut the cuffs off my shorts so that they ride high up my thighs. I touch my toes. I dab sticky pink gloss on my lips and my eyelids and my cheeks. I wear tighter t-shirts. I pick up the telephone and smile. I lock myself in the bathroom. I drape my legs over the chairs. I give him the finger.

He says, "Hand me that ashtray." And looks back to the window.

I hate June.

At the hospital, no one watched *Wizard of Oz*, which was playing on the tiny black and white wall-mount in his room.

Vivian drank black coffee from tiny paper cups. Pinched the pads of her fingers together. Pursed her lips. Paced. Her voice rose and fell. Hasty cigarettes. Hands fluttering. She said, "Goddamn, these bathrooms are the pits." And smoothed out his bed sheets.

He sipped apple juice. He asked the nurse for a kiss. He asked for banana cream pie. He asked for June.

When she finally arrived, he was practicing his X-ray vision. He said, "Let me guess. White lace."

June crossed her arms. "What the fuck is this?"

"It was an accident." Vivian's voice was already beginning to bend, a poorly tuned instrument.

"Is that June?" His eyes focused.

"It wasn't a fucking accident. Nothing's a fucking accident."

He said, "Let me guess. Black lace."

"Garret, shut up," Vivian snapped. And, "June, he doesn't know."

"He knows exactly." June leaned into his gaze, her dark blue eyes sparking. And spat, "You're pathetic. You're fucking pathetic."

And then the minister came.

June.

"She's gone out," I say. "It's Edie."

He hands me a magazine.

The girl is blonde. Sleepy-eyed. Bare skin. Sticky sheen. Lips budding, give me an *0*.

He says, "Now, that's a set of spinners. You need to get yourself a pair. Are you there, God? It's me, Edie."

The day he tried to die was the same day that Duchess got hit by a car. We found her later, lying limply on the street, just a few doors down. Her tongue hung loose. Her eyes were open.

June bawled. I bawled.

"For Crissakes," Vivian muttered, eyes bloodshot. "It's only a damn dog."

Duchess was June's mixed-breed mutt. She came with June and Vivian when they moved in three years ago.

The day they pulled up, wheezing station wagon loaded – *to the tits*, he said – June stacked her boxes in the corner of her room and refused to unpack. She kept saying that she wanted to go home.

Vivian said, "June, we are home. Look at your nice big bedroom."

It was my bedroom. But I had to switch because June was developing.

He took June shopping. He took June to the drive-in. He took June to the skating rink.

He said, "Edie, you've got to learn to share. A girl needs a father."

Vivian said, "June, what's wrong with you? Say thank you."

June said thank you.

Vivian said, "June, what's wrong with you? Give Garret a hug."

June gave him a hug.

"It was an accident," he said, each time he pushed open her bedroom door while she was changing.

"It was an accident," Vivian concurred, stirring her tea. But she bought June a lock.

"Don't you look nice!" He'd admire, and snap June's bra strap.

"Oh, Garret." Vivian, chopping carrots or wiping down the taps, would roll her eyes. "Grow up."

Duchess got hit by a car because the front door was swung wide open. Avulsed, like the gap left by a knocked-out tooth.

We never use the front door.

The television was on, *People's Court.* The gold chair was empty.

In the kitchen, the taps were running. The telephone was bleating, off the hook, receiver resting awkwardly inside one of Vivian's slippers. And a chair was overturned.

I sidestepped the broken glass, the puddle of water. Made a sandwich. And sat down on the living room couch. I sat very straight. My toes tingled. I took a bite. I took another bite. Perfect half-moons.

"Edie! Edie!" It was Vivian's friend Valerie, the loose cannon with the lousy luck. "There's been an accident. We've got to get June and meet Viv at the hospital." She turned off the taps. She put the receiver back in its cradle. She righted the spilled chair. She grabbed me by the hand. Mascara slime was pooled in the inner corners of her eyes. Her hair was frizzed in the humidity. And she smelled like gin.

We got into her rusting grey hatchback with the burgundy interior and the stink of strawberry air freshener. My skin stuck to the seat. She lit a smoke. Told me to hold my seatbelt tightly in place so no one would know that the buckle was broken. And said, "Let's blow this pop stand."

We didn't know it was Duchess we'd hit.

The fuzzy dice swung wildly with each corner she took. The sun-scorched cans of diet cola rolled violently. When we got to the high school, afternoon classes had just resumed. But June wasn't in class.

June was smoking cigarettes behind the Dairy Queen.

June.

She says, "I wish he'd fucking died."

I say, "I wish you'd die."

She pauses, mid eyeliner, and stares me down for a minute. She says, "What the fuck do you know, anyway." And turns back to the mirror.

I step hard on her foot.

She says, "Edie, fuck off!"

I fuck off.

The sound of Nancy Sinatra floats in from the living room.

"I want to come."

"You can't." She splashes Love's Baby Soft on her wrists, her ankles, behind her earlobes and between her breasts. And offers me a sip of the warm can of beer she's stolen from the pantry.

I dangle off the side of the bed, roll her Magic 8-Ball back and forth along the floor.

She blows a set of smoke rings. Gives herself a last-minute glance in the mirror. And double-checks to make sure her bedroom door is locked. She says, "Stay in here tonight."

And crawls out the window.

I stare after her. Pale blonde head bobbing down the street. She pauses, adjusts her halter-top. And continues.

I curl up in her bed. Shake her Magic 8-Ball. *June.* Footsteps creaking. *June.* The doorknob jiggles. I ask the Magic 8-Ball if I'll be pretty. *It is certain*, it says.

June.

"I'm not June," I say, screen door slamming behind me. "I'm Edie."

Sitting in the gold chair. He takes a long sip from his lowball glass. Eyes fixed. He says, "Edie." It's diaphanous. He runs a finger along his lower lip. "Come here."

I walk through the honeyed lamplight, the soft cloud of cigarette smoke.

He takes another sip. He says, "Gimme a spin."

I twirl.

He whistles. "Aren't you something." He pulls me to him, sits me on his lap. Presses my hand to his unshaven jaw. Cloudy-eyed. He points. "June has a beauty mark right here." His fingers graze my breast. "How about you?"

The screen door slams.

I jump.

His hand drops.

June's eyes are blazing.

"June." His smile is soft and humid. "We were just talking about you."

"You sick fuck." She grabs me by the hand so hard it hurts. He's saying, *June*, and I'm saying, *Dad*, and she's saying, *Edie, shut up*.

She locks the bedroom door behind us.

She shoves me out the window first.

The Night Is A Mouth

It begins with wetness: around the eyeballs, under the arms, between the thighs.

In the belly of the heart there's a pump that spits it out.

The wetness is want and the want lacks direction. Not to mention, its smell is a stink.

It's one of those nights.

The sky is a cluster of purple grapes. Plump. Swollen. Cloying.

If you were to bite into a grape, you'd choke on the size of its seeds. While you're gagging, the seeds will find a way. You won't.

There are two girls. They are made of math and orexia, an appetite for equations.

Gravity ($F = GMm/R^2$). Momentum ($p = mv$). Acceleration ($a = Dv/Dt$). Velocity ($V = d/t$). Inertia ($I = \int r^2 \, dm$).

At their feet is a flood.

In apartment number five, the toilet is clogged.

The water, just shy of spillover, shimmies.

Plunger in hand, hand on her hip, Gold leans against grievance and stares down the bowl.

In the stillness of stuck waters, a shadow in the shape of a twin sharpens. And the girl in the bowl dares Gold to come closer.

Gold scoffs.

The girl scoffs.

Gold narrows her eyes and models a yawn.

The girl models a yawn.

Pissed. Gold climbs every mountain. And at the drugstore, with its musty grey and its sting of rubbing alcohol, its expired film and its expired cough syrups and its dusty collection of enema kits and scratch-and-wins, Gold pockets a curling iron without getting caught.

The girl's not impressed. She stares at Gold as though Gold is average.

Gold's ears begin to burn. Out of the corner of a gritty grey eye, she sizes up her adversary.

Comely curvature. The girl is bold, bottomless. Density weighted with suggestion.

In the back of Gold's throat, a lump blooms. It tastes like acquiescence. She grips the toilet tank for balance. And gropes for refutation.

But there are no under-eye circles or compulsions. There are no split ends or second thoughts.

The plunger slips from Gold's fingers. She sinks to her knees and wraps her arms, a concupiscent hug, around the bowl. Gold and the girl lick their lips.

From the galley kitchen with its pale plum walls, its jam smears and its juice spills, K's voice comes calling. "Gollld!"

It sounds like a fly looking for somewhere to land.

Gold swats. And skims. Her chin. Her lips. The slightly upturned tip of her nose.

"Go-ollld," K singsongs. Propped up on her elbows, face cupped in her hands, she's staring at her reflection in the dulled chrome of the toaster. Fingertips pulling skin past socket bones. "Go-ollld!"

Gold dunks. And there are no high-pitched petitions because there is no K because there's no apartment number five. There's only this engulfment, this sensation of singularity.

K's eyeballs begin to parch. She drops her hands and shudders.

Suddenly, there's a gap. Water levels retreating, Gold's wet head hanging in the cold air. The shock is unbearable. The shame is cacophonous.

K steps away from the counter. Straps on a pair of scarlet stilettos and lifts her arms, lazy wings. "Go-llld," she honeys, and begins to step in slow, uneven circles. "Oh, Go-llld!"

Gold dives. Headlong, she crams herself into the bowl. Bottomless. Begins to gulp. The water rushes up her nose and down her throat. Flooded, love or its likeness. And Gold begins to gag.

K reels and topples. Limbs askew. She stares at the ceiling with its squashed spiders. Stretches, spread-eagled. And through the bread crusts and empty cola cans, she begins to fashion an angel out of the trash. "Gollld!"

Lungs aching. Gold splutters, wrests her sopping head from the bowl. Eyes swimming. Ears ringing. Room spinning. "What!"

K pauses, mid-angel. "I'm bored."

Gold struggles to catch her breath. And looks back to the bowl.

The girl stares flatly from its bowels.

"Fuck this!" Gold slams shut the lid, wings the plunger at whatever it'll hit.

Bull's-eye. The elegant bottles of perfume – pleasing curves, coloured glass – which Gold routinely thieves from the high-end department store with its designer boutiques and its classy stink – stumble from their shelf above the toilet, and shatter.

Satisfaction. It grabs Gold by the hips, slips her the tongue. She dallies for a minute. Then storms out.

The living room that's the bedroom that's the hallway is in one of its moods.

It bites at Gold's ankles. It nips at her earlobes. It tugs at the pockets that poke past the racy rise of her snug cut-off jeans.

She kicks her way past its leaning lamps and knee-high stacks of dirty dishes, its tangle of dress-up clothes and dental floss and candy bar wrappers, K's collection of broken tube televisions.

The floor won't stop following her.

And the wheeled crate that's for stashing hard feelings beckons.

Gold gives it a recalcitrant shove.

It smashes into the curio cabinet that contains K's collection of artificial birds with their realistic feathers and lonely eyes. Upended, lid loosened. The screams that have been stuck inside the crate tumble free and start screaming.

Gold throws herself into the aubergine armchair with its busted springs. And says, "You flushed your fucking underwear again, didn't you?"

K, languishing in the crimson flush of the sofa, doesn't bother opening her eyes. "I was tidying."

Gold glowers, swats at a scream eddying in her periphery and leans forward, twists her long dark hair into a tight tail. Wrings. Toilet water trickles through her clenched fingers.

"They're at it again," sighs K. She means the naked people in her head. They have a lot of sex. "Oh, man." She shoves her hands down her tight red tennis shorts. "I haven't seen him before."

The phone begins to ring.

Gold tilts her head and taps, an unsuccessful attempt to clear her waterlogged ears.

"Now I see you," says K, fingers curled like binoculars. "Now I don't." Binoculars balled into fists.

Gold pinches herself.

A scream catches K's eye. She grabs but misses.

The rats, with their fistfuls of cheese and macaroni, barely look up.

Gold stands. And cuts a rapid clip for the phone.

This time, K's ready. She lunges and snatches, pulls the scream to her ear. It's from the time she lost her keys because she lost her purse because she forgot she had one when she dashed after Royal who'd just called her a slut because the bartender had smiled and slid her a double. Her eyes grow glassy.

Gold hauls the receiver off its wall mount.

"Hello?"

"Gold, it's your father."

"My father's dead."

"Maybe so, but even still, I'm calling, right?"

Gold gnaws at a fingernail and leaves room in her silence for burden of proof.

"When you were small, you refused to walk. You used to drag your knees along the sidewalk on purpose. You liked the smell of disinfectant that followed.

"Once, you chipped your tooth on a hard c – you were trying to swallow the lie you'd just told.

"Also, you have a small scar on your left temple from the time you threw yourself from the trellis out back. You were trying to prove a point. The point was you were not afraid. We carried you inside and hung your head over the sink while the blood fell. You cried but you did not cry. You cried only because you couldn't believe you'd misjudged your angles. Since then, you've learned to gauge better.

"But you still hesitate when looking both ways, lest something barrel into you head on."

Gold is sold. "What do you want?"

LISA FOAD

"Your mother's on a rampage. She'll likely call you, and when she does, she'll probably tell you I'm a cheat and a liar. I'm not. She did not catch me having sex with a prostitute in the garage. We were just talking. Also. I've never stared at anyone's tits but your mother's. And. The day we were at the grocery store buying steak for the barbecue we didn't have because that woman with all the bracelets bent over, that wasn't my hard-on in my pants. I was holding onto it for a friend.

"It gets lonely here, Gold. Sometimes I feel like all I've got are the magazines I hide under the bed."

Gold picks at the painted molding that trims the archway that leads to the kitchen. Shiny flakes the colour of molasses.

"I've got needs, Gold.

"Your mother, she doesn't understand. All she wants to talk about is cooking and cleaning and why I've begun lifting weights. There are things she doesn't need to know."

Gold discovers a splat of pink bubblegum stuck to the sole of her silver peep-toe stiletto. It's still warm and it smells like cream soda.

"It's the way she shushes me when she's on the phone. It's the way she locks the bathroom door when she's in the shower. It's the way she puts away my shoes and my coat and the books I'm reading. It's the way she steals the covers."

Gold picks at the gum till it peels. Rolls it, as worry, between her fingers. And tacks it to the wall, a soft pink signet.

"It's the way she flushes the toilet when I'm talking to her. It's the way she wants to know what I meant when I said *that*, and where the hell I think I get off and who the hell I think I am. It's the way she never lets it be about the weather. It's the way she turns over at night.

"It's the little things, Gold. Speaking of which, did I mention that every single morning, I scatter fresh flowers across the front porch? Only her favourites: snapdragons and dahlias, roses and lilies, aquilegia and hibiscus.

"Gold, I need you to do something for me. Go to the window and wave. I'm at the payphone across the street."

Gold does, phone cord stretched as caution tape.

Beside the walkway that's called a park, where the kids play with sticks and empty potato chip bags and steal each other's bikes, is the shop that sells liquor and car batteries. And beside that is the payphone.

Gold's dad waves again.

Gold doesn't.

"That was nice. You look great. Can I come up?"

"No, dad. The place is a mess."

"Right, right. Okay. Listen, Gold. You're a good girl. I love you very much. Maybe even more than your mother."

Gold wonders if he knows he's talking to this Gold and not the girl in the toilet.

"You know, she left us once. She took the keys and she got in the car and she left. For hours or days, I can't remember. You screamed the entire time."

Gold sighs. "No. That was you that left."

"Right, right. Well, never mind, then. The point, Gold, is that I could've. But I didn't. I made a commitment."

"Dad, I've got to go. The toilet's clogged."

"Right, right. But listen, Gold. If you ever find yourself sitting in a city made of hunger, cut its heart out or it'll eat yours. No joke. And Gold, if you talk to your mother, tell her I love her. Tell her that I didn't do anything wrong. And tell her that if I did, it's partly her fault. Because we're a team."

"Dad—"

"Okay, okay. Bye, darling."

Seconds later, the phone rings. Sure enough, it's Gold's mom.

"Gold, it's your mother."

"My mother's dead."

"Yes, but Gold, I have to tell you something. Your father is a cheat and a liar. I caught him fucking a goddamned prostitute in the goddamned garage. I've thrown him out."

"He told me."

"Son of a bitch! Always beating me to the goddamned punch. What did he say? He denied it all, didn't he?"

"Mom, I've got to go. The toilet's clogged."

"You know, he's been sleeping in the goddamned car in the goddamned garage. You wouldn't believe the smell. It stinks of stale sweat and denial and fast food and bullshit and shit-for-brains and good-for-nothing. And also, Poison. Which is what the hooker was wearing."

"Mom—"

"Honey, I'm right here.

"You know, he keeps leaving me anonymous notes that pledge love and loyalty, ask for forgiveness, maintain faultlessness, and also threaten suicide. His handwriting is the pits.

"I throw them out with the rest of the trash: his socks, his ties, coffee grinds and the fruit that's rotting. But he digs through the garbage and he finds the notes, which are crumpled and stained and running with ink and the sour wet that swims at the bottom of the bag. And he wrings them out. And suns them dry. And he irons them flat with his palms and the heels of his feet.

"And he tapes them to the windows, so that when I'm doing the dishes or towelling off or checking on the neighbours or wondering where the hell my newspaper is and where the goddamned hell my life went – when I'm driving around the block in that goddamned piece-of-shit car – there he is, saying, 'Mistakes were made,' and, 'I'm sorry if you are.'

"I've had to knock out all the windows. You wouldn't believe the mess."

"Mom—"

"Gold, honey, I'm right here.

"You know, he's been trimming the hedges and watering the lawn and hosing down the driveway and yelling, 'Yehllo!' to the neighbours.

"And he keeps clipping the flowers in my garden. He leaves the blooms in wilted piles on the front porch. There's nothing left but headless stalks and headless stems and the absence of colour. It's a metaphor, and it's killing me.

"Sometimes, I leave him supper at the side door. I don't know why."

"Mom—"

"Gold? Honey. *I'm right here*. What is wrong with this goddamned phone?" Her mother's voice trails off and the receiver and Gold's ear get three good whacks on the countertop.

Gold begins to headache. She tries to pace but there's nowhere to go.

"Twenty-nine goddamned years. And this is what I get. Before we got married he used to slick back his hair with his saliva. I should've known."

Gold idles.

"You know, he left us once. He took the keys and he got in the car and he left. For hours or days, I can't remember. You screamed the entire time."

"Because you were trying to leave. You fought for the keys. He won."

"Gold. *Honey*." Her voice is shirty. "I am trying to tell you something.

"When I died, I learned how to swing a hammer and drive a nail in so deep that nothing, not even blood, comes out. The force of impact made my eyes water and the water in my eyes made me realize that I still had pain. I took the pain and I spent it on a case of diet cola. But it didn't make me feel any better.

"And I realized that my pain was anger and my anger was fear and my fear was grief and my grief was all your father's fault. And your father's faults made me feel even angrier, so I swung again and again and again, until my eyes stopped watering and I had nothing more to lose.

"Except I realized that I had lost your father because I failed, and that I failed because your father failed me.

"Now, I don't feel a thing but the weight of his mistakes.

"And everything looks like a nail."

"Mom—"

"I know, honey. You've got to go. But one more thing. When I died, I wasn't leaving you. I had to go be with me. These are the best years of your life, Gold. Discover your formulas. Then abandon them."

"Mom, are you in the shower?"

"I just can't seem to get the smell of him off me. Listen, Gold. If you talk to your father, tell him to stick it up his ass. That I've never been happier. That I miss him."

Gold hangs up the phone and heads for the kitchen sink to scrub her hands of residue. She twists the greasy faucet knobs on and on and on.

The pipes screech and whine and the tap hisses, sputters, then bursts, a furious spurt that spits ill will at Gold's hands as she picks at the dried yellow gob that crowns the squirt spout of the empty bottle of dish soap.

Gold spits the feeling right back.

But the sink, with its sluggish drain, wins.

"Fuck." Gold twists off the taps and jabs at the congested trap with a fork.

The phone rings again.

Eyes rolling, Gold gives her hands a half-assed swipe across the dark blue denim within which her hips are suggestively cinched. And grabs the receiver. "Stop calling me! I don't give a fuck who did what. This, that – you're dead, for fuck's sake!"

"It's me."

"Oh." Gold's shoulders sigh. She tilts her head, spies the fifty-dollar bill that's been slid under the front door. "Hang on." She drops the receiver, which twists and bounces and bobs. Aimless.

At the window, Gold leans, forehead to forearm to glass.

There are the high-rises. There are the shops that are for styling hair and fixing shoes and renting porno. And the shops that, boarded up, aren't for anything. There's the shop that sells liquor and car batteries with the payphone out front.

And there he is, where he always is. In the walkway that's called a park, where the kids play catch with balled-up cheeseburger wrappers and get hit by cars. He's standing beside the tree upon which all the dogs pee. In his hands, he holds winter. It's straining against the teeth of his zip-front trousers, the muggy ply of his palms.

With her right hand, Gold drags her tube top down to her waist. And presses her soft tits to the glass.

He reaches into his pants and begins to stroke.

There are no birds. There are no flowers. The days shorten, suddenly. It makes Gold sleepy. She stifles a yawn.

In the kitchen, K is rifling through cupboards and drawers.

Faster. Faster. His jaw slackens. His tongue is a thumb that has fattened and purpled.

In the closet, K is pushing past coats and clothes and shoes and bird shit and holiday wrap and candy bar wrappers and dreams they've given up on.

He pulls out his cock. And comes. Sharp neon white spurts.

Gold feels pregnant and backs away. Hand cradling her smooth belly, she wills herself to miscarry. And turns. And trips.

Over K, who's on all fours, rummaging through a gnarl of garter belts and sweat-stained t-shirts. Fanning through the pages of musty books. Overturning potted plants and coffee cups. Looking for Royal again.

"There's this math equation I'll never understand," K says, voice muffled, head under the armchair. She emerges with an old take-out container in hand and sits back, haunches to heels. Dumps the box of its contents.

Nothing but chicken fried rice.

She tosses the container and looks to Gold. "It has to do with longitude and latitude. You know those lines?" Thumb and forefinger pinched together, she forges a misshapen circle in the air. "Halfway around the world, what time is it?"

"It's a difference of twelve hours." Gold flops onto the sofa, kicks up her heels.

"Ahead or behind?"

"Travelling west? Or east?"

"What does it matter? Halfway is halfway."

"And twelve hours is twelve hours."

"Wait." K's forehead furrows.

"There's a date line in there."

"*Exactly*. So how come we can't go back in time?"

"That's not math. That's sci-fi."

K stands up. "You be twelve midday. And I'll be twelve midnight."

Gold rolls her eyes. "We'll never meet."

"Then this is all wrong. Let's start again."

Gold cocks a brow. "I've got an idea."

In apartment number five, the toilet is clogged.

The water, just shy of spillover, shimmies.

Plunger in hand, hand on her hips, Gold leans against lamentation and stares down the bowl.

"Grievance," says K.

"What?"

"Grievance. Last time, you leaned against grievance."

"Well, this time I felt like leaning against lamentation."

"You can't do that," K protests.

"Why not?"

"Because. It was my idea. In the first place, I mean."

"This is boring," says Gold. "Grievance."

"I feel sick," says K.

"You always feel sick," says Gold. And picks up the other fifty that's found its way under the door.

Once the knocking begins, nothing feels good.

Gold tosses. Gold turns.

All of the doors inside her head are swinging open and shut. She crawls under the bed. She reaches for K. There is no bed. She shuts this door. It flies open. She shuts that door. It flies open. She holds onto K harder.

In the push and the pull of the doors is the sound of violence. It gusts and it gales, and inside of its bluster is a whisper that whispers the word, *gold*. She buries the whisper that's a word that might be her name in the small of K's back.

The knocking keeps knocking.

She fucks three of K's brothers, the hot ones.

The knocking keeps knocking. It knocks at Gold's knees. It knocks at Gold's elbows. It knocks at Gold's guts. Gold starts screaming but the sound is silent. Into the silence, the whisper that whispers the word, *gold*, climbs. She finds the closest cliff and jumps.

Gold's eyes snap open.

The pitch is the blackest.

Bolt upright, Gold feels for her hands. They're clutching her throat.

Across the walls, in the glow that's the palest because all of the streetlamps but one are faulty and failing, the shadows bloom and menace. Like usual. There's the whirring stammer of the fan. There's the nattering of the rats. There's the lulling roll of K's breath, her head on Gold's lap, arms curled tightly around asylum. And there's the knocking.

The shake in Gold's shoulders slows, and the choke that's the hold of her hands softens. She blinks. Eyes sticky with sleep.

And spots the cliff from which she jumped.

And in behind it, the whisper that whispered before she jumped.

The knocking keeps knocking.

Riled. Gold scales the cliff. The air is thin and the view is miserable. She tugs her tube top up over her tits. Hair matted with hard work and bad sex.

At the door, Gold fights, flips the dead bolt against its will. Grabs the crystal doorknob and yanks. At the catch of the chain lock, everything shudders – the door jam, the walls, and the musty oil paintings with their fatigued flowers, loosed petals, stilled life, lying in defeat at the base of each bouquet – except Gold. She stumbles backwards, doorknob detached and in hand. Doves flutter.

Two boys. Their eyes are made of cloves. Their suits are serious. Their nametags are noisy. Their necks look like new. "Hi. We're here to help."

Gold considers the gulf of possibility that, bound by their weak jawlines and dimpled chins, has been blunted beyond belief. It stales her stomach. She slams the door but it bounces back.

The boys smile.

Gold doesn't. She tosses the doorknob. And heads for the bathroom.

K begins to nightmare. That the sky is a cluster of purple grapes. That she's choking on its seeds. That the seeds will find a way. That she won't.

In the small of her back, there's a whisper. She grabs it, grinds hard against it. Comes to just shy of satiation. Clammy sheet twisted between her tingling thighs.

In behind the chatter of the rats is a soft panting.

K squints, picks up the shaft of light that's spilling in from the front door. She adjusts her sticky tennis shorts. And gets up.

Briefcases pinned to their crotches. Eyes, as welts. "Hi." They gulp and pat down their cowlicks. "We're here to help."

"Do you know Royal?" Hand on her hip.

"No."

"Are you plumbers?"

"No."

"Do you know anything about frenzy or spasm, effusion or emission, gushing or spurting, release and relief?"

"No."

"Well, what then?"

"Well, we know about high points and low points."

"Like peaks and climax?"

"And abysses." One boy adjusts his tie.

"And flooding." The other boy adjusts his tie.

"Common ground."

"Second comings."

"Well, why didn't you say so?" K jumps so joyously her tits fall out. And unlatches the chain lock.

Gold has to pee.

She's leaning against the bathroom wall with its cracked sapphire tiles. Eyeing the chipped azure toilet with its smashed shut lid. Arms crossed, one silver high heel bullying a stack of magazines – true crime, celebrity gossip, *Guns & Ammo*. K steals them from the laundromat with the tepid dryers, the wheezing pinball machine, the loiterer with the lewd hand gestures and licentious eyeballs. Once, Gold knocked him in the head with the can of cola she'd just wrested from the defiant pop machine when she realized he'd intercepted she and K's spin cycle and swiped the yellow satin underwear that Gold had just swiped from the second-rate lingerie shop down the block. Now, he sits in the corner and stares, one restless hand conspicuously ransacking the space below the table, while Gold – seated atop the noisy washing machine, arms and legs crossed – stares thornily back.

From beyond the door with its broken lock, Gold can hear the sound of searching.

"Do you like camping?"

"No," says K. "But I appreciate a well-pitched tent."

"So do we. Do you enjoy baking?"

"No. But I admire a stiff batter, a nice rise. How about handguns?" K inquires. "Do you like to shoot?"

Gold thinks about biting the bullet.

"Well, aim is important. Safety first."

Sights set, Gold barrels through the congestion of jasmine and sandalwood, jonquil and plum, ylang-ylang and amber. Flips open the lid. The girl's right where Gold left her. That solicitous invite, that black hole. Gold pauses. Gold grasps. Gives the toilet a hasty flush.

The water whirls, obscures the girl. But the bowels choke. And the girl swells declaratively in the bloating waters. Unflinching. She makes a steady climb.

"Fuck!" Gold throws a towel round the base of the bowl. Between her thighs, a warm trickle. She shoves her hand between her legs and hips trembling, holds tight. Grabs the cloudy glass cup that sits next to the crumpled tube of toothpaste on the chipped blue pedestal sink. Ditches the scruffy toothbrushes. Hand sodden, thighs glistening. She unzips. Yanks her cut-offs to her ankles and squats. Cup in sight, Gold lets go.

"Boo!" It's Gold's father. He's been hiding behind the shower curtain.

Gold startles and for a second, misses the cup. "Dad! What the fuck?"

"I just wanted a hug."

"I'm peeing."

Grudgingly, he turns away. "Say, did your mother call?"

Gold finishes up, shakes. Winces at her wetted denim.

"What did she say?"

Gold dumps the contents down the sink and rinses the cup. The basin backs up. "Oh, for fuck's sake."

"Did you know she's begun wearing animal prints? Smoking the occasional cigarette? Did she mention that she threw me out? That I'm living in the garage? That before this even happened – of course, nothing happened – she was already making tea for one? Did she mention the flowers, Gold? The flowers! I'll kill myself, I swear."

"Dad, I've got to go." One hand on the doorknob, legs geared to hightail it.

It's hard to look good in this room. With its mashed violet walls, its wide angles.

Gold and K, however, have got it beat. They don't wear peach or salmon or foam. They ring their eyes in black and more black. And they exfoliate.

Not the boys. Slug-lipped. Pale, like unbaked loaves of sourdough. Thin, like capability that's been mixed with water. And cramped, like they've been sitting in jars too long.

Between them, the coffee table, cluttered with bottles of hot sauce. Sticky necks, crusted caps. One of the bottles, overturned, is seeping.

Before this, Gold and K had had a contest. They'd contested rejection.

"I feel sick."

"You always feel sick."

"I can't keep anything down."

"You keep everything down. You hold onto it and squeeze until it strangles. You refuse to let go. Look at Royal."

In her head, K murdered Gold. And, with her hands grabbing hold of her knees and the need to be right, she leaned forward and did her best to prove Gold wrong.

"That's just saliva."

"No, look." K pointed an insistent finger. "There's a bone."

"That was already there." Gold nodded at the assortment of chicken wing bones that littered the floor.

Another slim stem sailed through the air. Nearby, a cluster of rats were dipping celery sticks in blue cheese, delicately slipping the greasy grey meat off their drumettes.

"It's me who can't keep anything down." Gold dug through a snare of glittery nylons and speaker wire, and extracted a chicken ball. "The moment I chew, there's a fight." She popped the ball in her mouth and got to work. With difficulty, Gold swallowed. "See?" She pointed.

Sure enough, the descent down Gold's esophagus was marked by agitation.

"Oh, God," said K.

"Just wait," said Gold. She cut a swath through a jumble of fashion belts and satin opera gloves, and leaned forward. The turbulence ascended swiftly and, with finesse, expelled from her readied mouth. "Now, that's vomit." She pointed to its rusty browns, its pale apricots, its exclamatory reds.

K, thoroughly invigorated, shivered. "That *is* vomit."

But it wasn't. The pulp had begun to quiver. Tiny limbs and scaly pink tails emerged and elongated. Ears budding. Snouts broadening. The rats opened their eyes and blinked, paused briefly to groom their handsome bellies, and scurried off.

"Is that where they keep coming from?"

Gold rooted for another chicken ball and tossed it at K, who dodged.

From behind a stack of foreign language dictionaries, a rat poked its head, whiskers twitching, and nosed the air for direction.

"I can't eat. Especially that. It's so old."

"Rats won't eat bad food. They're non-emetic." Gold scratched lazily at the soft skin of her outer thigh before reaching to remedy the riding-up of her lacy black underwear. "Besides, all our food is old."

"Old in the fridge is different than old on the floor."

Gold shrugged. "Fine."

They searched the fridge for provocation.

Licorice. Beef jerky. Abandoned take-out. Pickles. Pots heavy with stiffened oatmeal, pasta primavera. Slickened lettuce. Olives. The giant jar of pitted sour cherries K just had to have.

Gold piled the lot into K's cradled arms and her own. And reached for the hot sauce. "It aids in digestion."

"Are you sure? Maybe it's an irritant."

"Who cares?" Gold said. "Either way." And slammed shut the fridge with her hip.

On the coffee table, Gold assembled their options. And doused the opening round in hot sauce. "Don't touch your eyes," she warned. "You'll go blind."

K grudgingly browsed the take-out, most of which was from the shitty diner down the block with its oddball liquors and its pallid wall-mounted pictorial menu. She reached for the leftover grilled cheese, took a tentative bite. And spit.

"That doesn't count," Gold said. "That's just spitting out chewed food." She swallowed a piece of licorice. Vomited. "See?" Polished off a forkful of pasta primavera. Vomited. "See?"

"Show-off," K muttered. She searched Gold for signs of exertion and fluster.

But Gold's lips were plump and glossy. Her dusty eyes sparkled. Her cheeks were flushed ripe. And her dark waves tumbled lavishly about her breasts.

K thought about biting into Gold's delicious head and eating it like an apple. Instead, she reached for a fry. Chewed carefully. And swallowed. Minutes possessed the weight of hours. K grew crestfallen. "Do you think Royal misses me?"

"I think Royal's an asshole."

K promptly vomited.

"Not bad," Gold offered. "The colour scheme's nice. But you're still holding back."

K swallowed a spoonful of oatmeal. "Do you think Royal wishes it was me sitting next to him at the movies?" And puked immediately.

"Oh, that's a good one," Gold nodded.

Blushing, K bit into a strip of beef jerky. "Do you think Royal can still smell me on his fingers?" And puked immediately.

"Now, that – that's almost a ten."

"Do you think I'm pretty?" K puked again. "I feel so fat." K puked again. "I hate this freckle." K puked again.

"I hate my eyes," said Gold. "They see things."

"I hate my heart," said K. "It says things." A violent expulsion. Dazed and weak-kneed, she looked to Gold for congratulations, then back to her outpouring. Her smile fell and her eyes grew wide with anguish. "It looks like Royal," she whispered.

Gold leaned in for a better look.

"Don't touch!" K shrieked. She tucked her hair behind her ears and slung herself closer, searching. "In his eyes, I see myself. The reflection is uncanny."

Palms sweaty. Gold said, "I especially hate the girl in the toilet."

"She looks a lot like you," K murmured.

Bedlam threw Gold forward with such force that her elbows bruised. Before her faint body, a swamp of silver whites, copper reds, restlessness and hard *c*s.

"Oh, man." K whistled. "Look at that gold leaf detail."

Gold could hardly believe it herself.

"And those hard *c*s!" K marvelled. She cast a dull eye at her own emesis. "Mine sucks." And looked back to Gold's expulsion. Her voice softened. "It's like you're crying." She reached to give Gold a hug.

Gold shook her off. "But I'm not."

Exhausted. They curled up together in the makeshift bed that's mostly made of the floor.

"I feel sick," K said.

Gold rubbed K's stomach and K got hard. "Not again," Gold sighed. "Do it yourself."

K tried. "I can't even come."

Gold tried. "Me neither."

And twined, they fell asleep.

Inside the brown-bricked four-storey walk-up, with its crumbling cornices and its dead language for eyes, is the yellow-green light. It flickers. It buzzes. It stings. It burns. It oversees the insides.

There are the brass mailboxes with the busted locks and the doors that gape like struck-open mouths. They're stuffed with the things that no one wants: misdirected mail and junk mail, single socks and resentment.

There's the plaster ceiling with its sweeping swirls and cresting spikes, its cracks and its seeping brown.

There are the cobwebbed corners where the small speakers, through which muzak used to be piped, are hitched.

There are the pale walls with their peeling skin that's the colour of yearning that has yellowed. They're pitted with holes left by fists that frustrated. Blotted, also, with the smear of oily fingertips.

There are the fatigued floors with their slanting give, the threadbare carpeting with its whirling browns and mustards and melancholies.

And there are the crumbling stairs with the magnificent banister, its flamboyant decay.

Up three flights, past the stink of urine and regret, and the clutter of chewed pen caps and bloodied bandages, crumpled religious tracts and squelched condiment packets, down the hallway with its big, bold doors with their big brass numbers that hang askew, is apartment number five. Inside, there is wetness. The wetness is want and the want lacks direction. Not to mention, its smell is a stink.

"Tell us about Royal," say the boys, and adjust the lapels of their serious suit jackets.

"I don't have a picture but he looks a lot like release plus relief, or restlessness plus reason, or something that belongs right here." K gestures to the space beside her on the coffee table. "His anger is sadness. And his sadness is the saddest. He makes me feel fatal. Which makes me want to live forever."

"He sounds a lot like God."

"Yes," sighs K.

"That depends," Gold counters. "Is God more of an ass man?"

"Stop that," says K.

The boys blush. Look to their neatly clipped fingernails. And clear their throats. "Where do you feel it?"

"Here."

"Yes."

"And here."

"Yes."

"And here."

"Yes!" The boys slip suddenly to the floor, noses mashed against the smooth pink shells that are K's kneecaps. Hands groping, elbows twisting, they scramble to right themselves. Tug at the tight collars of their crisp white dress shirts. Say, "Ahem."

Gold rolls her eyes.

"What about here?" The boys point stiffly. "Does it feel like there's a burning in your bosom?"

"Oh, yes," says K. She feels for her bosom. "*God*. It feels like a fire." She feels up her bosom. "*God*. I'm burning and burning." She slivers open one eye. "*God*. It's the hottest." And yanks down her tube top.

"Oh, God," say the boys. Around their eyeballs, there is wetness.

"Yes, *God*," says K.

"Does it feel like there's a light inside you? A pillar of light inside of you?"

"Yes!" heaves K. "Yes!" heaves K. "Yes!" Then her shoulders slump. "No." Lower lip quivering. She opens her eyes and the tears roll hopelessly, gutter through the narrow channel between her breasts. "He comes and he goes."

"He always comes and goes," says Gold.

"We can help you find the light," say the boys. "We can help you keep the light. A constant companion, you'll see. You'll feel the light."

Gold can feel the light. It's hot and white and sharp. She balls it up inside her fist, jams it between her legs. And coughs. Luminescence. It emanates from her heart-shaped mouth, engulfs the room. Hot. White. Sharp.

"See?" say the boys.

"See?" says K.

"Fuck that," says Gold. "I can't keep anything down."

When Royal left, the rats stopped hissing and K began looking.

She began looking for things to fill up the space between her body and the front door and the door next door to that. She brought home with her the suffocating humidity, nutritional supplements, pamphlets detailing how to live with incurable disease, and more broken tube televisions. The sound of all the children crying consoled her greatly. But she was wary of its heart, so she left it sitting in the dumpster with the dirty diapers.

She said, "He's coming back."

She said, "He must be coming back."

She said, "I'll bet this is a test." She stayed up all night studying. Still, he didn't come.

She gathered up the stringy hairs he'd shed and fashioned a promise ring. She couldn't believe her eyes. "Look," she said to Gold. "It makes my finger look more like a finger." And pretended to hold his hand by resting hers in one of the holes he'd slugged in the wall.

She said, "Was that the door?"

It wasn't.

She said, "Was that the phone?"

It wasn't.

She said, "I'll bet he's hiding." And checked the teapot. When Gold looked at her quizzically, K took a tone. "Don't you think the closet is a little *obvious*?"

She began looking over her shoulder, behind her back. She began looking over her shoulder, further back. Walking in circles. She kept bumping into things and acquired many bruises.

One day, she knocked herself out. When her eyes fluttered open, she found herself on the sofa, a cold compress on her forehead, hand in Gold's.

Gold looked at her gently. Opened the crate that's for stashing hard feelings and said, "Scream." But because it was all she had left, K said, "No." And Gold said, "Scream," and K said, "No," and Gold said, "Scream," and K said, "No," and Gold said, "Scream," so K screamed at Gold. "Good enough," said Gold. And closed up the box.

K knew better than to seek solace from her mother. The last time she called her mother was the day K came of age.

Her mother, who was busy admiring her gin-soaked teacup, said, "I'm not interested." And then, "I'm sorry, who did you say you were?" And then, "Oh, K. Aren't you a peach? I never could stand your whining. I knew there was a reason I stopped taking you to the mall." And then, "K, darling, I'm glad you called. Have you any money? I'm all out under the couch." And then, "This isn't a good time. I just haven't the stomach for it. Call your father." And then, "Jesus, K. I've told you a thousand times. I'm not sure who your father is." Her mother gave K a list of possibilities. And said, "When you find the bastard, you tell him he owes me a lot of money!"

K dialed each number but none were in service.

So she waited. And in the rolling spoil of dusk, she canvassed the bars with their stink of beer and hopelessness to see if she could find him. Men who wanted to be her father asked her to sit on their laps. But none had her cheekbones or any money. Plus, they kept calling her Kay.

So she stopped. She stood on the sidewalk. She wiped her neck where the men's breath had lingered. And she began to walk. Her feet moved faster and faster, especially while she was being chased. She was running before she was chased.

The boys lick their lips. Loosen their ties. "It's never happened quite like that before." Their Adam's apples bob. "Will you show us how you did that?"

Gold licks her lips.

"It's awfully hot in here," the boys stammer. And rash-cheeked, remove their serious suit jackets.

When Gold's parents died, she didn't cry. In fact, she felt annoyed. She was sure it was a trick, a bid for attention.

At the funeral, Gold wore snug blue jeans and aggressive red lipstick.

She delivered a eulogy. "My mother and father liked not being needed. Because it allowed them to need more and more and more, until there was no room in the room for anything else. 'Gold, fetch me

THE NIGHT IS A MOUTH

a soda. Gold, how's my waistline? Gold, what's a three-letter word for help? Gold, there's a spider. Gold, how's this colour on me? Gold, I hurt my finger. Gold, I love you. Gold, I said, *I love you*. Say it back.'"

In response to the pastor's look of surprise, her mother whispered, "She's on her period."

But Gold wasn't on her period. "At first," she tapped her impressive spike heel, "this made me feel necessary. But the necessity with which I needed to feel necessary made me feel sick. And I realized I didn't want to die.

"Thank you, Mom and Dad. You've taught me how to kill."

After the funeral, Gold sat atop the rusting monkey bars at the park across from the porno theatre. She suddenly felt very tired. She suddenly felt very lonely. She smoked a cigarette. And cracked open the fortune cookie she'd been given on her way out of the church. *It's not advisable to leap before you look, but that may be all you have time for.* Gold rolled her eyes and hopped to the ground. Tossed the cookie to the pigeons. And walked away. Throat swelling. She swallowed. She fought to keep the feeling down. Her feet moved faster and faster.

Just then, her father drove by and said, "Gold, honey, get in the car. I just need to talk."

Gold ignored him and tramped ahead.

He drove slowly alongside her, chattering incessantly. "That went well, don't you think? Good attendance. The Bellows came – and we don't even like them. Did I look all right in the casket? I was too pale. Your mother, though, she was something. I was bonkers lying next to her. It was all I could do, I'm telling you, Gold."

Suddenly, the need Gold had learned not to need came riling up her throat and all over the sidewalk. Hands and knees, Gold studied the tiny rats rubbing up against her forearms, begging for belly rubs.

Her father eyed the rodents. "Jesus. They have *got* to clean this city up." And, checking his reflection in the rearview mirror, said, "How's my hair? I've been growing it out. Now I'm not so sure."

She looked at her father with his fine-toothed pocket comb.

She looked at the rats with their pink eyes and big ears, their contented chirps.

She decided the need needed her more. And, rats in tow, left it at that.

The building is restless. It rumbles, a queasy stammer that sours the air. The windows rattle. Walls shuddering. The rats start screeching and the screams start screaming.

The boys clutch their knees. Their knuckles whiten. Their eyes saucer and begin to spin.

"It's nothing," K declares. "It's just —" but the rumble's become a roar and her voice drowns in the ruckus.

The building staggers. Lurches.

The boys lean forward and grip their spindly shins. Mouths churning, "I swear," and "I promise," assorted last minute entreaties.

And the stomach of apartment number five careens wildly into the throat, where it hovers for just a second, before plummeting violently.

Everything hits the floor with a clatter.

And the boys promptly lose both their dinners and their bladders. They look up, shame blossoming along their necks.

"It's okay," K comforts. "We do it all the time. And anyway, that was just the building settling. Last week, we were on the fourth floor. Now, we're on the third."

"Soon we'll have to move," says Gold, and pets the fluffy copper-eyed cat that's fallen through the ceiling and landed in her lap. It mews delicately.

When Gold and K met, it was love at first sight because it was not love at first sight.

The night was a mouth and the mouth was full. It was full of bad feelings and feeling sorry, and also, the blues, which were rabid.

Two girls. Breathless. They met, by mistake or not, at the corner of danger and not danger, which is the corner where the people with their cream-coloured clothing and their mouthfuls of mint gum roll up their car windows because they're afraid of the skinny people who hold out their hands and ask for help.

They did not like what they saw. In the inner corners of their eyes, devastation seething. In the apples of their cheeks, desperation rouging. In the gullies of their throats, jealousy starving.

All around them, the things that were beautiful were asleep. They should've been asleep.

They stared hard for a long time.

"Would you care for a cherry?"

"I can't keep anything down."

"I can't get anything out."

They began to like what they saw.

And fingers laced, they walked. They walked in the direction of elsewhere, which was a direction that neither would have anticipated or could have planned.

Past the pawnshops and sex shops and tattoo parlours, the butcher shops and the video arcade. Through the schoolyard strewn with empty bottles of lemon gin and peach schnapps, birds crudely cut out of construction paper. Past the railroad tracks and the people sleeping inside newsprint. Past the kids playing with bricks, the men drinking out of paper bags, and the feral cats sleeping with their eyes open under the cars that hadn't yet been stolen. They walked past the shops that were in the middle of stick-ups. And the signs that said *For Lease*, and *Final Score: Satan Zero – Jesus Won*, and *Spare a Dollar*.

They climbed on top of the night. And, cross-legged, they sat. They looked into the future. It looked much the same as the present and the past, the things they couldn't know, the things they didn't love. They agreed that everything that could be built could be torn down. They didn't know where to begin.

"Tell us about your clogs," say the boys. Struggling to regain composure. Stuffing their crisp white dress shirts back into the waistbands of their crisp black dress pants. Patting at their cowlicks. Under their arms, there's wetness.

"The toilet is clogged. The sink drains are clogged. The tub drain is clogged. The things in between are also clogged. My stomach. My throat—" K pauses, confused, for the boys are looking elsewhere.

With their eyes split open, whites whelming. "Holy smokes," they whisper. Jab the air, tremulous fingers furnishing direction. "It's a ghost!"

It's just Gold's dad.

Annoyed, K rolls her eyes, waves dismissively. "It's just her dad."

He's hiding, hardly, behind one of the lamps that are leaning. He smiles sheepishly, waggles a few fingers. "Hi, there." Shoulders hunched, weight shifting from one foot to the other. "Pretend I'm not here."

"My eyes. My ears—" K watches the boys watch Gold abandon the magazine through which she's been skimming and, eyes flashing, long legs gunning, close the gap. K clears her throat, raises her voice. And yanks down her tube top. "My heart, my head—"

"Dad."

He's now idling awkwardly against the wall. Wide eyes pitched skyward, fingers fiddling with a ding in the plaster. He begins to whistle.

"*Dad.*" She gives him a sharp tap on the shoulder.

"Oh, Gold!" He jumps and, shock-eyed, a stylish display of counterfeit confusion, lifts a shifty hand to his heart. "You startled me." Pat. Pat. "How are you doing? Nice place you've got here."

"What do you want?"

"Right. You know, listen." Hands fumbling. "It's just—" He inadvertently knocks the beaded lampshade off its base.

Gold snatches the shade, shoves it back atop the glaring bulb. It hangs lopsided, a hat tip.

He shoves his hands in his pockets, jangles loose change. "I have this feeling that your mother might call, and if she does—"

Sure enough, the phone rings.

Gold and her father lunge for the wall mount. Fists flying.

The boys clap their hands across their mouths and duck.

K raises her voice over the din. "Our telephone line, our tear ducts, our ability to accept things."

"Speak for yourself!" Gold yells, and wrests an arm free of her father's grip, cracks him in the jaw.

K drops her voice. "There's a girl in the toilet. She looks like Gold."

"I can hear you!" Gold hollers and knees her father in the nuts.

K drops to a murmur. "Our ability to swallow. Our capacity for satiation. Our willingness to want and be wanted. It's the difference between caring and caring less. The dishonesties that live in our hands often conspire against us."

Gold snaps her neck, eyes glinting. "I can still hear you!" And gets belted in the head with the receiver. Goes down. But she holds one of her father's teeth in her hands.

"Hello?" He claps his hand over the mouthpiece and, wild-eyed, mouths, *It's okay. I got it. It's her.* Turns away. "No, no, I know— No, listen— No, don't hang up—"

While Gold rubs her head, struggles to get her bearings, K hastens. "Our front door. Our apartment. Our bodies. No release. No relief. It's relentless. Hard feelings. Boredom. *God.* Plus, the sky is clogged with purple grapes. The night is choking on it. Not to mention," she shoves her hand down her shorts, and holds up two glistening fingers. "This wetness. It's everywhere."

Nickels for eyes, dress pants pitching. The boys make rash grabs for the crimson throw pillows and attempt concealment. Tug awkwardly, insistently, at the decorative tassels. And say, "We're sorry for your losses."

"Bullshit," says Gold.

"Stop that," says K. She turns to the boys. "And?"

"And absolute truth can help."

Gold rolls her eyes. "There's no such thing. There are only things we can agree on."

"She's right." Gold's dad gives her a thumbs-up. And turns back to the phone.

Gold stares the boys down. Density weighted with suggestion. "The toilet is clogged. The drains are clogged. The building is sinking. It feels good to come."

"It *does* feel good to come," says K.

"But the second coming is worth waiting for," say the boys.

"We haven't even gotten through the first one yet," K whines. "Oh, this unrest, this cramping." She rubs her hand between her thighs. "It's driving me mad."

"God can take all that away," say the boys, straining. "But you have to be open. Willing to receive."

"I'm open!" K lies prone on the coffee table. "I wish to receive!"

The boys stutter. "It involves a laying on of the hands."

"Yes, lay on your hands!"

The boys dig their fingers into the bloody red of the sofa. Voices cracking. "You'll need to make a covenant."

"Well," K gives them a sly smile, runs a hand over the curve of her breast. "I won't tell if you don't tell."

The boys gulp. "Remission through immersion. A saving ordinance."

"Don't make me save it!" K wails.

"No kidding," Gold seconds. "We've already saved everything that we care to save." She gestures to the broken tube televisions, the furniture culled from the trash, the screams.

From the kitchen, Gold's dad pops his ruffled head. "Ah, guys? Hello? I'm on the phone. Keep it down."

"Not to mention," Gold continues, "we don't care much for the present, but we care even less for the past and the future."

"I care for the past!" K says. "I've always wanted to start with the end of time and work my way backwards. I would change everything."

Gold cocks a brow. "I've got an idea."

In apartment number five, the toilet is clogged.

The water, just shy of spillover, shimmies.

Plunger in hand, hand on her hips. "Fuck this," says Gold. And rams the rubber mouth into the bowl. Asphyxiation, the girl surges. Choppy waves. Gold squints, braces herself against splash-back, and pumps harder. The pipes begin to gurgle and moan. The claw foot tub belches, and the sinks erupt. Rowdy dregs.

From the bowels of the building, a raunchy growl rises, winds its way through Gold's guts. Small tremors. She hammers the bowl harder. The building sways, bricks crumbling.

Harder.

"Gold!" K screams.

Mid-plunge. "I'm coming!" Gold hollers.

"Me, too!" K exclaims.

"My eyes!" scream the boys.

Gold's dad is exasperated. "Please! I am on the phone!"

Plaster cracking. Windows shattering. Pipes bursting. Gold gives the bowl one last plunge. The building shudders. Keels. And collapses.

Gold opens her eyes. The light is everywhere. Hot and white and sharp. Streaming in through splits and breaches, cavities and fissures.

Hands sticky. She picks her way through the debris, the murky overflow.

On the coffee table, K is lounging, curvy-lipped and loamy-eyed, one lazy hand rooting through the rubble. "Has anyone got a cigarette?"

The boys don't say a word. Slouched on the sofa, two soggy slices of bread.

Gold points to the wet spots on their crisp black dress pants. "Revelations."

The boys begin to cry.

"There, there," says Gold.

"There, there," says K.

They stroke the boys' hair. Cup their cheeks. Say, "Shhh," until the boys fall asleep.

Gold's father emerges from the kitchen's remains. Brushing the dust off his shoulders. "We got disconnected." Adjusting his collar. "But it went *really* well." He retrieves his pocket comb, runs his tongue along its teeth and coifs. "I think I got her, Gold." Covers his mouth. "Sorry," he whispers. "I didn't realize they were asleep."

"I'm fucking starving," K murmurs. "My mouth's all dry."

"Me, too." Gold's eyes sparkle, quartz crystals. She disentangles from the gawky limbs of the boys. Stretches.

Gold's father tiptoes through the wreckage. Whistles. "Goddamn."
He turns to Gold, beaming. "That's my girl."

Outside, Gold and K look around. Fingers laced.

All around them, the buildings are dead, hearts cut loose.

The streets are flooded.

The night looks like new.

Lacunae

There's this picture of us. *It's to die for.* We're being swallowed. Light everywhere. Our eyes are closed. Our mouths open. There is no cure. Our lips are touching. There are no witnesses.

We're trying to remember what comes next. We think about ordering out. Sushi? Thai? But our hands shake. *Do or die.* We pretend to die. Touch up our eyeliner. And make some toast.

Look, to the light. There's a gun. The gun's loaded. Not loaded. We wonder if we're seeing things. *Dead ringers.* We get the spooks. And turn up the music.

Killer. Our moves are killer. No one wants to tangle with us.

Bored. We practice piano, our runway walks. *Knock 'em dead.* Swan dives. *Dead on.* And watch disaster films. Calculate our chances. Tornado? Tsunami? "Dead meat," you say. And readjust your bangs.

Joie de vivre.

We pretend we're on a street corner. Dovercourt and Argyle. The houses are taller, skinnier than we remember. Lean, just left. Time stops. For a second, we're dead. We can smell it. We think about running. Instead, we close our eyes.

Wait for wind and things to die out.

I open my eyes. In your hands, you hold a vertebra. "Thoracic," you say. I worry it's mine. "That's going to scar," you say. Smear at a tributary of blood. "Tastes real nice." The phone rings. I give it the finger. Open my eyes. The hallway's dank. Emergency lights flickering. I wonder where you are. *Dead ends.* I call your name. And open my eyes.

We try to remember what comes next.

The Words

The sky was the colour of a dirty dishcloth. And it was heavy as a wet tea bag.

Underneath its weight, the people were waning.

Walking into streetlamps. Guzzling colas. Popping painkillers. Straining to wrest free from the sticky air that stretched as cling wrap across mouths and noses. Fainting, dull thuds like dominoes. The sidewalks were a mess.

From her sixth-storey suite, the girl with the boring blue eyes watched without watching. Abstracted. She did not think about throwing herself off her Juliet balcony with its ornately bowed iron bars. For in her hands, she held an envelope. Lavender-scented. She inhaled deeply. Delicate fingers, she removed the invitation from its jacket. And pressed the paper shell to her lips.

Another body plummeted past the gossamer of fancy that veiled her eyes. Seven storeys, it hit the ground with an unforgiving splat.

The girl eased the envelope into her mouth. And, sucking gently on the soft crumple, she leaned a fraction forward. Cast a faint gaze over the balcony's edge. And murmured tenderly, "Goodnight, Mr. Dewitt."

The bells trembled and chimed.

The shoe man didn't bother looking up. He could smell the feel of her already. Sugared, a squishy sweetness, sticky and warm. Glutted, he rolled over. It was delicious.

The girl clapped her hands over her ears and grit her teeth. "How do you stand it!" The heat was unbearable. The sundry scents of polish and wax, dye and stain, dizzied her senses and she reached for the counter to steady herself. Uncapped her water, took a woozy sip. Then she remembered her manners. "Hi, there." She smiled widely.

Inside of her mouth, past the tidy row of twinkling teeth, he could see that a field of flowers had wilted and died.

She reached for the bag slung over her shoulder. And knocked over a rack of leather conditioners and lotions. "Oh, dear. I'm so sorry." She bent to attend to the spill and knocked over a rack of mink oils. "Oh, dear. I'm so sorry."

In his head, he concurred. She was very sorry. With her bobbing blonde ponytail and her tiny gold earrings, her dewy-eyed blink, and her voice, pale, the colour of cake batter. Her timid white sundress with its eyelet lace bodice, the white heels in which she teetered. The thin gold charm necklace, its dangling letter *A*. He watched her bend over, felt the pull of the panty lines that announced, a little too loudly, her heart-shaped bottom. He rolled over again.

She wobbled precariously, a loose tooth. And fell. Face-first, she took with her the rack of water guards and stain repellents that the strap of her purse had inadvertently snagged.

Buried under the pile of shoe supplies was a whimper.

Her white satin panties winked at him. He rolled over again. And hopped the counter to assist.

Two hands flailing, she struggled for modesty. Blinking back soppy tears. His eyes were the colour of mint leaves. "I'm so sorry." She hiccupped. "I'm so sorry." She hiccupped again. She looked to the calloused hand he'd extended. It was the size of a bowl. She placed hers inside.

He yanked. The force threw their bodies together with violent certainty, and he found his lips up against the lobe of her ear, the gorge of her neck, the wisps of sweat-stuck hair, that sweet yeasty bakeshop scent. She began to chew her gum faster. He felt her hand strain against his. He tightened his grip. She swallowed her gum. He let go.

"Thank you," she whispered, eyes averted. "I'm so sorry."

"I know."

She took a deep breath and unwittingly swallowed the stink of his underarms. She was about to recoil. But remembered her manners. And smiled widely. She reached into her bag and extracted a pair of shiny gold stilettos in need of new heel tips. "When will these be ready?" Her voice feathered with hope. "I have a party to attend. I have my invitation right here."

He glanced at the creamy glitter-flecked card stock with its elaborate gold cursive: *A late-night garden party. Cancel your Sunday morning appointment with God and come spin the bottle with Frances.* He sucked the air through his gold-capped teeth.

She startled at the sound.

"Check back tomorrow." He slid her a moist business card and watched her tottering tiptoe take her out the door. The bells tumbled. He wiped a fleck of glitter from his hand. And said to himself, "Soon."

Outside, the girl paused. Disoriented.

All along the skinny winding streets, cars were jammed bumper to bumper. Horns honking furiously, while the streetlights blinked disorder. The church bells rowdily declaring hours that were not hours, halves that were not halves. And the river was roiling.

All around her, the people were careening. Stocking up on canned goods. Engaging in impromptu curbside sex. Holding anticipatory funerals. Digging holes in the dank earth and crawling, white-eyed, inside.

She threw her head down and hastened, sidestepping bodies and empty cola cans, abandoned children.

Up ahead, an old woman was on her knees. Tearing off her clothes. Her heaving breasts sobbed while her fingers flew feverishly through benediction. At the sight of the girl, the woman balked. "There are two hands," she shrilled. "Squeezing the life out of you." Her glass eye rolled about its socket. Her snarled grey hair wound wildly through the wind that wasn't blowing. "You'll be dead before sunrise. And if not, then the sunrise that follows. And if not, then the sunrise that follows. And if not, then the sunrise that follows."

"I— I'm sorry," the girl stuttered. Pinwheeled. And ran.

The pale yellow princess telephone rang.

With a soft hand, the girl collected the receiver. "Hello?"

"Have you seen the papers?"

She hadn't.

"Armageddon is coming."

"But there's a party on Saturday."

Her mother issued a contemptuous snort. "We'll see about that." And, "Oh, for heaven's sake. Where's that damned toilet tissue? With the lights out, I can't see a damned thing." She lifted a coy hand to her slick silver blonde upsweep. "I guess it doesn't matter. He is everywhere, after all."

"Who is?"

"God, Adelaide. God is everywhere. Good grief. You'd think you were raised in a barn. Honestly. You make me feel like a failure. I can hardly stand it. It's a wonder I don't drink." She cast her gold-shadowed eyes skyward. Winked. And conjured, a swift whisper: "*It works if you work it so work it 'cause you're worth it.*" She gathered her bearings and the sheer back-seamed pantyhose that were bunched around her classy spike heels. "I've taken to tinkling with the lights out, darling. It's called humility. A healthy sense of shame goes a long way. Now. Where were we?"

"Armageddon."

"Armageddon, indeed. Have you watered your plants?"

"No, I—"

"Called your grandmother?"

"No, I—"

"Taken out the trash? Revised your résumé? Booked a pap?"

"No, I—"

"Honestly, Adelaide. Ever since Frances broke off with you—" she *tsk*ed, "you've been a lump." She adjusted her leather pencil skirt and with great satisfaction, surveyed her reflection in the wall-to-wall mirror. "Indulge me, Adelaide. How is it that you managed this forfeiture?"

It was during, of all things, a round of Truth or Dare.

First, Evangeline dared Frances to slide his hand up her silky pink skirt. She said, "That's right. Yes. Right there." When he finally withdrew, his fingers boasted a glossy sheen. And in his pants, enthusiasm sprouted.

Then Aberdeen dared him to join Evangeline in the closet for Seven Minutes of Heaven. When he came out, he was milky-eyed and starving.

Then Millicent dared him to break up with Adelaide and date Evangeline instead. He didn't think twice. He said, "Adelaide, you're dumped." He pulled the promise ring from her finger and slipped it onto one of Evangeline's.

It was humiliating.

To be fair, however, Frances was always up for a challenge.

When he excused himself to attend to his blue balls in the bathroom, Evangeline placed her newly ringed hand upon Adelaide's demoted one, and leaned in. Her shiny dark hair hung in long, thick swirls and her alabaster skin glowed. She dipped her voice into a honey pot and said, "If you weren't so tight, Adelaide, maybe the decision would've been more difficult." Then she let out a peal of laughter within which Aberdeen and Millicent threw themselves and rolled about, flush-cheeked and febrile.

Adelaide shoved a chunk of hair in her mouth and began to suck.

The girls tittered. "It's too late for practice now."

Adelaide jumped up and ran down the hall to the Polynesian-themed bathroom. It was empty. She tried the Vegas-themed bathroom. It was also empty. The old Hollywood bathroom, however, was locked. She banged at the door, rattled its knob. "Frances! Frances, please!"

The door finally opened.

Evangeline, with her petulant lip and her mussed hair, narrowed her eyes. Her fingers toyed with Frances' earlobe. She said, "Do you mind, Adelaide? My boyfriend and I are having a little *down* time."

"Oh, I'm so sorry," Adelaide rasped weakly, and spun on her heel. She held in her tears until she'd cleared the front door. And ran, a sobbing wreck, all the way home.

It was true that Frances was very stupid. Most of their conversations never made any sense.

"That's dumb."

"What is?"

"I don't know. It just is."

And so it went.

Initially, Adelaide had thought that he must be very profound, that it was she who was very stupid. But there were only so many times that she could have the same conversation. Not to mention, how quickly his favourite game – "Look!" he would exclaim, hands behind his back. "No hands!" – wore thin.

Nonetheless, there was something endearing about his gaping obtuseness within which all the girls wanted to drown. "Those eyes!" they'd squeal. "That jawline!" And grind themselves hard against their chairs during third period, slyly slip their wetted underwear into his hands as they passed him in the halls. Their attentions made Adelaide feel like she had something of value. So she cupped it in her hands and held onto it as tightly as she could.

When her mother heard the news that it was over, she gave Adelaide a cool once-over. "Hell in a handbasket." Then she rolled her eyes. "I can't say I'm surprised. Landing him was luck of the devil. Honestly, Adelaide. What will I do with you? Never mind a facelift. I need a damned faith lift!"

She'd been wild about Frances.

"Aren't you a doll!" she said, when first she laid eyes upon him. She toyed with the pear-shaped diamond nestling seductively in her plump bosom. "I could eat you." Later, at dinner, she snuck a hand under the table and leaned forward. "Call me Heloise, darling. Or—" The plunging neckline of her blouse gave way to the lacy leopard-print brassiere underneath. "Hellcat, if you'd rather." She winked, rubbed the sole of her stiletto up against his calf. "Oh! Aren't I a naughty thing!"

They got along famously.

"That's dumb," he'd say.

"What is?" Her mother, always up for good scandal, would lean in, tenterhooks.

"I don't know. It just is."

"Oh!" her mother would laugh richly. "It is, isn't it? *It really is.*" And slap his thigh, take a demure sip of the Drambuie that hid in her teacup.

Frances was a painter. Each painting looked the same. Impish scribbles in primary colours. "This is called *The Distance Between Time and the End of Time,*" he would say. "Here," he would point, "is Time. And here," he would point, "is the End of Time. And here," he would point, "is the distance between the two. And this right here," he would point, "that's me."

"Ooh," said the critics. "Ah," said the critics. "And so it is."

He painted one for her mother. He said, "This is called *The Difference Between Sleep and Sleeplessness.*"

"Brilliant!" she'd exclaimed, and squeezed his buttocks.

"Here," he pointed, "is Sleep. And here," he pointed, "is Sleeplessness. And here," he pointed, "is the difference between the two. And this right here," he pointed, "that's you."

"Oh my!" Her mother raised her diamond-ringed fingers to her jaw. "My cheekbones really could cut glass!"

That night, Adelaide tugged open the french doors that let out to the balcony. All across the city, small fires were burning in second- and seventh-storey windows. On the streets, the bandits were handing out glow sticks and the song lyrics to *Iron Man*. The people sang horribly. Voices cracking. Words dissolving. Gibberish.

Adelaide shuddered, shoved a chunk of hair in her mouth and began to suck.

A soft rustling noise wound its way round her earlobes. She looked down. Rocking gently back and forth amid her collection of orchids was a loose glass eye. Adelaide screamed. She kicked it as hard as she could, watched it somersault through the air. And slammed shut her french doors.

In bed, she stared at her party invitation. She found herself thinking of the shoe man's mint green eyes. She recoiled. But the eyes crawled into bed with her and against her will, snuggled inside her lids. And slept.

The next day, Adelaide telephoned the shoe man.

"Not today," he barked. "Maybe tomorrow." He loved the sound of her voice. He could hardly wait for tomorrow. He bit into a strawberry-filled jelly doughnut. The jam oozed, mingled with the powdered sugar that dusted his chin. He swiped a finger at the thick red juice and licked.

As soon as Adelaide hung up, the telephone rang. "Hello?"

"Have you renewed your passport?"

"No, I—"

"Taken your vitamins?"

"No, I—"

"Booked yourself at the hairdresser's? Given blood? Reread *Revelations*?"

"No, I—"

Her mother sighed. "Had only he given you the clap, Adelaide. Curious vexations, an atypical scent, a troublesome leak. Excess bleeding. Dysuria. That damned itch. *Excuse me. Does my cervix look irritated to you?* Honestly. You would get swabbed. You would take pills. You would not touch your eyes. You would be *fine*."

Adelaide couldn't bring herself to tell her mother that she hadn't put out. Especially given that Frances was hung like a horse.

In the bathroom, Adelaide yanked up her pale yellow sundress and hurriedly sent her pink satin panties to her ankles. Sat. And promptly screamed. There, on the white-tiled floor, just beside the toilet, was the glass eye. Adelaide scrambled. She turned off the lights. She pulled at her panties. And, in spite of the errant trickle down her thigh, she ran to the kitchen for a pot. She scooped up the eye, clamped the pot's lid in place and tossed the entire lot off the balcony. It clattered satisfyingly.

That evening, in the empty spot that sleeps beside her in bed, Adelaide gingerly laid out her party dress, a slinky black number with thin gold pinstripes, a plunging neckline, cap sleeves, a sash belt. It wore like a whisper, hot breath on the neck.

She could hardly wait. She imagined herself walking into the party. Heads turning. Tongues dragging. Hands hungry. Everyone, even Evangeline, fighting, slit-eyed and wet-lipped, to get Adelaide punch, to hold her hand, to neck with her in the closet.

Frances will feel so jealous. He'll throw himself at Adelaide's feet and beg for attention. She'll shush him, a slim finger to her lips. And tell him to meet her in the closet. *Heaven in Seven*, she'll say.

And in that darkened hole, amid the smell of fine Italian leathers, up against the silks and cashmeres, she will thigh-high her dress, resolutely wrap her legs around him. And she will put out.

He'll gasp for air, lose sight, all feeling. The tightest sex he's ever had.

Afterwards, he'll trail after her like a dog. She'll pat his big dumb head and let him squeeze her fine breasts in front of Evangeline, while slurry-eyed, he digs his tongue down Adelaide's throat, mining for meaning.

And Adelaide will leave, holding in her satisfied hands, his flailing heart and Evangeline's rouged humiliation. Carnivores will howl longingly as she saunters down the block, a fine blush on her cheeks, a purse full of phone numbers, the musky scent of all the people who brushed up against her with their desperate desire.

And that night, he'll telephone her obsessively until she finally picks up. And he'll say, "Adelaide, will you go steady with me?"

I'm so happy I could die, she thought to herself. *I'm so happy I could die.* She wrote the words down on her palm, lest she forget.

The next day, Adelaide telephoned the shoe man.

"Not today. Maybe tomorrow." He bit into a custard-filled doughnut. The thick yellow yolk squeezed deliciously; the chocolate icing cracked, a gooey smear on his lips. He licked his fingers and settled in to think about her thighs.

The telephone rang. "Have you called your psychic advisor?"

The next day, Adelaide telephoned the shoe man.

"Not today. Maybe tomorrow." He bit into a powdered doughnut. Marshmallow crème squirted everywhere. He admired the rising river levels, and settled in to think about sharing a bath with her.

"But I need them!" Adelaide wailed frantically at the dial tone. "My party is tomorrow!" And, slushy-eyed, she slipped the phone back into its cradle.

The telephone rang. "Have you at least made your bed?"

The next day, Adelaide telephoned the shoe man.

"Today's the day," he avowed. "After eight o'clock this evening. But before eight-thirty." And slammed down the receiver.

Adelaide's ears rang with excitement. She squealed and spun wildly about her suite. *I'm so happy I could die.*

The telephone rang. "Have you thought about taking up a hobby over the summer?"

"Not today!" Adelaide yelled. "Maybe tomorrow!" And slammed down the receiver.

She shivered. She paced. She executed a series of jumping jacks. She gnawed on a licorice stick. She ran laps around her suite. She panted.

She dusted the light bulbs. She flipped through a copy of *Our Bodies, Ourselves*. She rearranged her spice rack. She studied the invitation. Inhaled.

In the shower, Adelaide scrubbed with lemons and honey and nectarines. *I'm so happy I could die. I'm so happy I could die.*

She slipped into the skinny dress, knotted its flirty sash. She painted her lips slut-red. It made her feel illicit. She shivered. If she were the sort of girl who fucked herself, she'd grab a cucumber right now. *Now that's love*, she'd say, lids fluttering, eyeballs rolled skyward.

She slipped on her least favourite shoes, the scuffed red kitten heels, so that she could toss them into a trash bin later. And left the house. Aglow.

On her way, she paused at the magazine stand to buy some chewing gum. And bent to study the newspaper headlines. There were none. In fact, there were no words at all. *Mother doesn't know what she's talking about*, she thought, and rolled her eyes. *All of these papers are blank.* She held up a copy. "How much?"

"$1.50." The man adjusted his bowtie.

"But it's blank."

He shrugged. "It's the weekend edition."

Something rolled to a rest at Adelaide's foot. She glanced and met the ominous gaze of the glass eye. "Not tonight," she declared testily, and gave it a swift kick.

As she approached the tiny shoe shop that looked more like a shed, her stomach sank. Its insides were darkened, dead. And the sign was flipped CLOSED. Her eyes began to well and her lungs began to panic. She tried the door anyway. It didn't budge.

Adelaide burst into tears and sank to the shop's stoop. She slipped off her shoes, tucked her knees under her dress. And let the river with its garbled rush lull her to sleep.

She woke with a start and, eyes darting, fought for her bearings. The sky was a black eye. From her mouth, she dragged the chunk of hair she'd been sucking, and looked up at the shoe shop. Staring back at her from the window were her gold stilettos. Adelaide stood so fast her head spun. She tugged at the door. No yield. She hammered at it with her fist. No answer. She pressed her fingertips to the glass and stared desperately.

In the distance, she could hear the sound of a fête. She turned and squinted.

In the small plaza nearby, the cops were having a cop car party. Admiring one another's candy-coloured customized lowrider cruisers, with their tail fins and rear wheel skirts, their plus-size rims. Comparing auto body art, pinstripes and flames, airbrushed tits and ass. Bouncing, squad cars shimmying like stallions. Showing off their side to sides, their pancakes, their single- and double-pump hops.

The bass was booming.

Adelaide reached for her shoes but they were gone. She took off running. She hardly felt the pebbles that dug into the soft pads of her feet, the abandoned glow sticks that had long lost their charge.

"Officers! Officers!" she cried. And nearly wiped out on a used condom. "Please help!"

The cops were squishing their tallboys and cracking open new cans. They gave her an amused once-over. "No shoes, no service. Unless, of course, you'd like to service." They unzipped their pants. Laughed gregariously. And high-fived one another.

Adelaide pinwheeled. And ran away.

The mammoth white house glimmered, a jewel. It took up half the block.

At the front walk, Adelaide hesitated. She could hear the festivities carrying on in the yard around back. She spit out her gum. She checked her breath. She tried to clean off her feet. She smiled coyly. She smiled winningly. *I'm so happy I could die.* She took a deep breath. And lifted the heavy brass medusa head knocker. It thudded. She gulped. And felt something cold nosing around her big toe. She flinched at the sight of the glass eye. *Fuck off*, she hissed. And gave it a nasty punt. It landed with a thunk in the flowerbed.

A girl answered the door. She was dressed as a dragonfly. Four iridescent wings, a sparkling satin hourglass corset with matching panties, garter and stockings. Icy blue. Her shoulders dusted in glitter. She eyed Adelaide's filthy bare feet. "Invitation, please."

Adelaide handed it over.

The dragonfly narrowed her eyes. "This invitation is blank," she said in disgust. And slammed the door.

Adelaide gasped. It *was* blank. Somewhere along the way, she had lost the words. She scrambled through her purse. Nothing. She checked the soles of her feet. Nothing. She inspected the porch with its potted plants, its lovers' bench. She checked the front yard, the front walk. Nothing.

At the sound of Frances' voice, however, Adelaide, with a soft step, stole her way to the back of the house. The yard was breathtaking. Tiny twinkling lights were strung throughout the trees. The waterfalls spilled gently, their basins bedecked with floating pink flower blooms.

There were corseted dragonflies everywhere. Lighting sugar cubes on fire over shots of absinthe. Handing out spiked punch and skewers jewelled with cubes of grilled pineapple and mango and peach.

Everyone was laughing. Toasting their champagne flutes, their ginger martinis, their blueberry basil cocktails. It grew very loud. It grew very deafening. Adelaide shoved a chunk of hair in her mouth and began to suck.

"Lila peed her pants yesterday. *At the mall.*"

"That girl is hopeless. How about Carmen? She slept with Mr. Malone under his desk. She thinks she's pregnant. Whatever. Who sleeps with a fucking math teacher, anyway? Film studies, maybe."

"Speaking of, Lucy got caught jerking off with Mrs. Jennet's porn. Swear to god. Mrs. Jennet called my mother immediately. She said she came home early and Lucy was spread on the fucking couch. She said, 'That girl's babysitting days are over.' I mean, a person's porn is *private*."

"What do you expect? That girl is so bottom-tier."

"That's dumb," Frances said.

The girls gaped. "What is?" they pleaded.

"I don't know. It just is."

"*Oh my god!*" they screeched. "*It is totally dumb!*"

Adelaide rolled her eyes.

"Oh. My. God. Adelaide? Is that you?"

Adelaide found herself encircled by Evangeline, Aberdeen and Millicent, their riotous curls, their pretty pastel dresses, their matchstick heels. They smelled of peach blossoms and tequila.

"Yoo-hoo!" Evangeline hailed the crowd. "Look what the cat dragged in!"

"Please," Adelaide whispered.

"Adelaide is here. Sneaking about."

Heads turned. *Adelaide is here. Adelaide is here. Sneaking about.* The murmur rippled through the party.

"Oh, Adelaide," Evangeline sugared. "Don't cry. It makes you look even *more* precious."

Everyone giggled hysterically.

"Evangeline!" Adelaide whispered, her wet eyes wide. "Your mouth is bleeding."

Evangeline put a finger to her pretty pink lip. "Shit."

Adelaide watched the word slip from Evangeline's mouth and fly off.

Evangeline saw it, too. "What the fuck is going on?" But the words hardly made a sound. They leapt from her lips and ran away. "Oh my god. Can you hear me?"

Oh my god! Oh my god! Can you hear me? Everyone began to panic.

Adelaide watched all their words tumble down the block. She took off running, in hot pursuit. Behind her, the words that people were screaming fluttered and flapped. The glass eye found Adelaide and kept pace.

It began to rain. Great big sopping drops. The sky fell open.

142

The words hastened behind Adelaide. She stopped short and flattened herself against a tree. Out of breath, soaking wet. And watched the words stampede past. At the river, they gathered. Then threw themselves into the rapidly rushing water, to drown. Their screams were spine tingling, bloodcurdling.

Adelaide gasped, horrified. "This is a horrible place to die!" she wailed. And clapped her hand over her mouth. But the words were already gone.

The bandits offered Adelaide a cigarette.

"I don't smoke," she said. And watched those words make a run for the river.

"You might as well start. Armageddon is coming."

"Stop talking!" Adelaide screamed. And wondered what words she still had left. She lit the cigarette. Tears rolled down her cheeks.

Do something, her eyes pleaded.

"Why don't you?"

"I can't swim," she bemoaned. And clapped her hands over her mouth. Too late. The words darted and dove into the water. Imploringly, she looked to the bandits. *We can't just let them die here!*

The bandits shrugged their shoulders.

She rushed to the riverbank and fell to her knees, sobbing. *I'm so sorry! I'm so sorry!*

A swarm of words abruptly collided with Adelaide, caught her by the elbows, the hair. And charged ahead, carried her with them into the river. The angry black waters rose and she kicked and gasped and spluttered and screamed, fought to stay afloat. But the words that were drowning tugged at her ankles. And the words that were jumping landed on top of her, pushed her down.

Adelaide, flailing and fighting through the leaping words, pulled herself, with all her might, ashore. And unclenched her fist. In the palm of her hand, she held a word that she'd caught in mid-dive. Letters broken. The word was *now*.

Adelaide turned. And saw that the tiny shoe shop was lit up.

At the door, she paused. The sign had been flipped OPEN. And in the window, her shoes glittered. She bit her lip.

The shop went violently dark.

Adelaide gave the door a shove. The bells tinkled.

There was no answer.

She reached for her shoes. They looked brand new. She strapped on the shiny gold stilettos. Straightened. Pointed a toe, admired her foot in the small shoe mirror. And heard a noise. She spun around.

The shoe man was sitting in the corner on a small wooden stool. His gold teeth shone. He looked at her. And said, "Now."

But the word was already in her hand.

Acknowledgements

First and foremost, thanks to everyone at Exile Editions for the tremendous encouragement and support. In particular, I want to thank Barry Callaghan for his invaluable insight and brilliant counsel, the care and acuity with which he delved into and nurtured this collection. It was an honour to work with such a skilled writer and editor. I'm very grateful to Michael Callaghan for his diligence in detail and design. Many thanks, also, to Meaghan Strimas for her concentrated contemplation of the text, and Matt Shaw for the careful eye.

I'd also like to thank Sonja Ahlers for her gorgeous artwork and Jessica Eaton for all the pretty pictures, Lynn Crosbie and Tamara Faith Berger for their attentive reading of the manuscript, Simon Sykes-Wright for his exhaustive engagement with several drafts, and Zoe Whittall for deliberating early drafts.

The Canada Council for the Arts, the Ontario Arts Council, and the Toronto Arts Council provided generous financial support during the writing of this book. I'd also like to thank those editors and publishers who recommended my work for grants through the OAC Writers' Reserve program.

And warmest of thanks to my family and friends for the support, inspiration and mad love – especially Angie Holmes and Zoe Whittall, Sandy De Almeida, Joe Pert, Leslie Peters and Carolyn Gordon. And, of course, everyone at Lot 16, for giving me the room I needed to complete this collection.

An early version of "Violent Collections, Anxious Supplements" appeared in *Red Light: Superheroes, Sluts & Saints* (Arsenal Pulp

Press, ed. Anna Camilleri), and *Exile: The Literary Quarterly*. An early version of "Expulsion For Emetophobia" appeared in *Matrix*. An early version of "Here There Be Monsters" appeared in *Exile: The Literary Quarterly* under the title "The Package."